GW00598285

THE TIMEKEEPERS

BY

CHARLES MOORE

Charles Moore

Copyright Charles Moore, January 2006

British Library Cataloguing In Publication Data
A Record of this Publication is available
from the British Library

ISBN 1846850576
978-1-84685-057-8

Published January 2006 by

Exposure Publishing, an imprint of Diggory Press,
Three Rivers, Minions, Liskeard, Cornwall, PL14 5LE, UK
WWW.DIGGORYPRESS.COM

THE TIMEKEEPERS

BY

CHARLES MOORE

CHAPTER ONE

It was the sort of hot day when ice-cream vans did a roaring trade. One went past and stopped a little way up the road from where Jake Hepton was sitting on the grass verge. He got up, picked up his school bag, and ambled towards the van, which was now surrounded by a dozen or more kids from the local primary school. Halfway there, he stopped abruptly and checked his pockets. He cursed to himself as he remembered the earlier incident at school - the incident which meant he now had no money for ice cream. He glanced enviously at the crowd queuing by the van before crossing the road and heading for home.

It had been one of those days for Jake. A boring day at school, most of which had been spent day-dreaming at the back of the class. His lunch money had been spent long before the lunch break: the two pound coins he had in his pocket exactly matched the sum Patrick Snooge demanded to stop twisting Jake's arm behind his back.

Jake wasn't an unpopular boy by any means – he had as many friends as most other 16 year olds, and he was a key player in the school football team – but he was also one of Snooge's regular victims. If any of them told a teacher about the bullying, the arm-twisting got more painful, and the price of release doubled. Some of his victims had recently started muttering about how they were going to get back at Snooge, so it should only be a matter of time before the counter-plot was hatched.

School was often quite boring for Jake, especially as the exams approached. He was one of those rare pupils with an ability to absorb information effortlessly. Nothing ever needed to be repeated, and any attempt at revision was usually pointless. Nevertheless, he always tried to make out the work was as difficult for him as it was for his classmates, often by asking questions that he already knew the answer to. At least it ensured the others couldn't tease him.

It was a trick he had learned soon after starting at secondary school, when he had often been teased about being a swot or a teacher's pet. The teachers, of course, recognised his natural ability, and were happy to play along with the pretence.

Jake turned into Duckworth Close. The Hepton family lived at number 23, a detached mock Tudor property surrounded by a low, neatly trimmed hedge. The four bedroom house was easily large enough to accommodate Jake, his parents, his younger sister Alice, and his tortoise Speedy (although, strictly speaking, Speedy had his own purpose built hutch in the back garden). Duckworth Close was a quiet cul-de-sac on the edge of town, almost completely surrounded by fields which were now full of barley and wheat. A public footpath led from the end of the road to a copse of trees in the middle of the fields, where Jake had often made a secret den when he was younger. It was still his favourite place, but nowadays he went there just to relax rather than to build dens. Hardly anybody used the footpath, so Jake regarded the copse almost like his own private property.

As he walked down the road, he noticed Mr Walker at number 11 sitting in his garden under a big sun umbrella. Jake had always liked Mr Walker. He was a kind old man, who appeared to be totally content with his life. Even though he must be over eighty, his garden was immaculately maintained. The weed-free flowerbeds brimmed with a dazzling array of colours, and it looked as though he used nail scissors to cut the grass in preference to a lawnmower. An ornate pond, with a small fountain and a large number of goldfish, stood between the patio and the lawn. It was no surprise that Mr Walker had won the local council's 'best kept garden' award for the last three consecutive years. When asked by the local paper how he managed to maintain such a beautiful garden, he would always reply:

"Time is the secret."

"Hi, Mr Walker," called Jake cheerily.

"Afternoon, Jakey," he replied. "Fancy a glass of lemonade?"

Mr Walker was the only person in the world who called him Jakey. He would have felt like a clown if any of his friends called him Jakey, but he made an exception for Mr Walker.

"Some of your homemade lemonade?" said Jake. "I'd love some. I'll just drop my school bag at home and get changed. Back in a few minutes."

"Take your time. I'm not going anywhere."

Jake trotted off down the road to number 23, and let himself in. Nobody was home, and the house was quiet. Since it was Thursday, Jake's mum would be doing the late shift at the hospital where she nursed, and Alice would have gone to her friend Becky's house for the afternoon to do her homework. His dad, as the managing director of a local pharmaceutical company, rarely got home before seven o'clock and quite often worked much later.

Jake took off his school uniform, leaving it where it fell on the floor, and put on his favourite pair of shorts and the new Nike T-shirt that

Alice had given him for his birthday in May. His bedroom looked a bit of a tip, but then it always did by Thursday. By Saturday, it was almost impossible to enter. But he'd made a deal with his mum that he would always tidy it up on Sunday mornings.

Feeling much more comfortable now that he was out of his uniform, he locked the door behind him and walked back to Mr Walker's house.

"How was school today?" asked Mr Walker, once Jake had taken his glass of lemonade and settled on the other sun lounger.

"Pretty boring," said Jake. "We're revising for our exams right now, so we're not learning anything new. It sounds strange, I suppose, but I'm not at all nervous. Most of the work seems pretty straightforward."

"You always were a bright lad," said Mr Walker. "You pick things up easily, and you work hard. I don't reckon you'll have any problems."

"Well, I feel fairly confident, but I've got no idea what I want to do afterwards," said Jake. "I mean, most people have some idea what they want to do with their lives, don't they? Most of my friends already know that they want to be – accountants, doctors, teachers. I just can't think what career I want. I'm sixteen now, and I should have at least some ideas, shouldn't I?"

"Not necessarily," said Mr Walker. "Besides, what's the hurry? You've got plenty of time. You probably already know what subjects you prefer, and these exam results will give you an indication of which subjects you should concentrate on. That'll narrow down your options for university, and you don't have to decide on a career before then. Things will fall into place, you'll see."

"I hope so," said Jake, unconvinced. "It's just that – I wish I knew what I'm going to be doing in ten years' time."

"Well, even if someone could tell you that, you probably wouldn't believe them. Things change, lad. There's no point in worrying about it now. Take your time, and relax. I'm speaking from experience, you know. I didn't start my own career until I was around twenty five."

"And what was your career?" asked Jake, suddenly realising how little he knew about Mr Walker's life.

"I was an artist," he said.

"You mean all those paintings in your house are your own?" asked Jake.

"Most of them, yes."

"Cool."

"Thank you – if that was a compliment," said Mr Walker.

"Yeah, it was. I think they're really good. I never knew you did all that."

"Well, I was a bit like you, really." Mr Walker got up and took a few steps towards the fish pond. He picked a few food pellets out of a plastic box, and scattered them on the surface of the water. "When I left school, I had no idea what I wanted to do. I still had no idea after university, which was a bit more worrying. I wanted to travel, to see the world and experience life, but there aren't many careers that offer you those sorts of opportunities. So when I left university, I decided to go to Africa for a year. I spent a bit of time teaching English, and then discovered that I loved drawing and painting. There were so many things I wanted to remember – the wildlife, spectacular sunsets, amazing scenery – but colour photography hadn't been invented then. So I painted them instead." He walked back and sat down again. "I managed to sell a few paintings, and realised that I could actually make a living from doing something I enjoyed. I never got rich but, I tell you, I've had a wonderful life."

"So all your income came from selling paintings, then?" asked Jake.

"Most of it," said Mr Walker. "I inherited some money from my mother when she died about twenty years ago, and that enabled me to live a little more comfortably than before. Painting isn't an easy career, you see. It can hardly be relied upon for a steady income, but I didn't care in those days. As long as I had enough money for food and lodging, I was happy. Nowadays it's more difficult to live with that kind of philosophy, so I would never advise you to tread the same path. But if you were to ask for my advice, I'd just tell you to try to do the things that you want to do in life, not just the things you think you ought to do. If you don't at least try to do the things you want to do, you will always have regrets in later life. I don't have any regrets, and that makes me happy."

Jake thought about it for a minute. "Well, that sounds like good advice. You've got a nice house and garden, you've enjoyed your life, and you don't have any regrets. I hope I'll be able to say that when I'm your age." He looked at his watch. "Look, I'd better be off. Mum will be home any minute, and I'd better make it look as though I've been doing some revision. Thanks for the lemonade, Mr Walker, and the chat. I really enjoyed it."

"My pleasure, Jakey." He paused. "Tell you what, come over on Saturday afternoon, if you're not busy. There's something I want to share with you. It'll take some explaining, but I'm sure you'll pick it up quickly."

"What is it?" asked Jake.

"Not now, son. It's something quite important, and it's just between you and me. I'll explain on Saturday."

"Sounds intriguing," Jake said. "I'll come over after lunch then, and you can tell me all about it."

There was an enthusiastic spring in Jake's step when he set off for school on Friday. He had spoken to Mr Walker lots of times before – he had known him for sixteen years, after all – but their conversation the day before had been, well, more mature. Jake had learned something about Mr Walker's life, and had discussed some of his feelings about his own uncertain future career. But what did Mr Walker want to talk about on Saturday?

Again, he spent much of the day thinking about things other than revision. He knew he should have been concentrating on his school work, but he really couldn't get into it. He wasn't worried about the exams: he knew that he would do well, and he knew further revision was unlikely to make him do any better. He convinced himself that he would probably just tire himself out. Relaxation would be far better for him than cramming.

At lunchtime, he saw Patrick Snooge striding purposefully towards him. Jake put his hand in his pocket, and pulled out half his lunch money.

"Here," he said, as he tossed the coin on the ground by Snooge's feet. "I can't really be bothered to go through that again, and I'm sure you've got better things to do. I'm not that hungry anyway. Have a nice lunch!" And, smiling pleasantly, he walked off in the opposite direction, leaving Snooge completely perplexed.

Later that afternoon, with only enough money for a snack lunch, Jake decided to make himself one of his special treats when he got home. He opened the front and back doors of the house to encourage a through-breeze, and set about making a triple-decker peanut butter sandwich. Alice always called it disgusting but, since she wouldn't be home for about half an hour, Jake would be able to eat it in peace. He put the sandwich on a plate, and turned to the fridge to get a glass of milk. He turned back, and was shocked to see that the sandwich had disappeared!

9

He stood there motionless for a second. His eyes searched all around him but he couldn't see it anywhere.

This is crazy, he thought. He couldn't have dreamt he made the sandwich, could he? No, definitely not, he decided. The knife was on the side of the plate, and it still had peanut butter on it. And he certainly hadn't eaten it, since he was still starving. All he had done was turn around to the fridge to get the milk. The sandwich had vanished into thin air.

Rubbish, he thought. Sandwiches can't just vanish. There must be some perfectly logical explanation, but that didn't make the hunger go away so he made another triple-decker. He put the knife in the sink, and picked up the sandwich, savouring the sight of it. He took the first, huge, bite from one corner and reached for his glass. He froze, hand outstretched and cheeks crammed with peanut butter and bread. His glass was empty! He stared at it for several seconds, before forcing himself to chew and swallow, trying feverishly to remember whether he had drunk any milk. He was sure he hadn't. No, he definitely hadn't. The glass had been full just seconds before, and now it was empty. First the sandwich, and now the milk. I must be going crazy, he thought. He didn't know what else to conclude: maybe the heat of the day had got to him, or he was too tired.

He poured another glass of milk, and tried to think rationally. There was nobody else in the house. Maybe an animal had run in and out – a squirrel perhaps. But no, he'd have seen or heard an animal. Besides, a squirrel wouldn't have been able to carry a sandwich that size, let alone drink a glass full of milk. No, he decided, he must have eaten the sandwich and drunk the milk himself, simple as that. The human brain sometimes works in strange ways, as his biology teacher had said recently. Yes, that was the most rational explanation. He had done it himself, but he couldn't remember doing it.

Jake put it to the back of his mind. He went upstairs, changed out of his uniform, and went out of the back door, heading for the copse. He propped himself up against his favourite tree – a big old oak tree – and closed his eyes, savouring the peace and quiet.

He remembered about the sandwich and the milk much later, when he was in bed. But he was far too tired to work out any other explanation for what had happened.

He fell asleep, none the wiser.

CHAPTER TWO

On Saturday morning, Jake got up quite early. He didn't enjoy sleeping in late – unlike Alice – and preferred to chill out on the sofa, watching nonsense cartoons until it was time to go to cricket practice. There was no match today, which was just as well, since it was grey and overcast. After the heat of the last few days, there was likely to be a big thunderstorm. Shortly before nine, he walked the short distance to the cricket pavilion, and spent a couple of hours in the nets. His team was quite good: the boys all lived locally, and several attended the same school as Jake.

After getting home and showering, he went up to his room and did some revision for an hour, more to avoid any nagging from his mum than because he really needed to. It was a relief when Alice banged on the door, shouting that lunch was ready before thundering downstairs to get first choice of the crisps his mum had bought to go with the sandwiches.

Saturday afternoons were relaxed affairs in the Hepton household, especially if there was no cricket match for Jake to play in and his parents to watch. Jake's dad settled in front of the television, and was soon snoring contentedly, while his mother busied herself with household chores. Alice was back in her room, making up yet another dance routine and singing along to her favourite CD. Jake pulled on a pair of trainers.

"I'm going over to see Mr Walker, Mum", said Jake as he headed for the door.

"Okay, love" she replied, without looking up from her ironing. "You'd better take the umbrella – there's one in the cupboard by the front door."

It was raining quite heavily now, with loud thunder rumbling through the dark clouds overhead. No sitting in the garden this afternoon, Jake thought. He rang the doorbell and waited.

After no more than a few seconds, the door opened and Mr Walker stood there with a welcoming grin.

"Jakey, hello, come in, come in," he said. "Nice to have a bit of rain, at last, but no point in standing around in it."

Jake folded down his umbrella and left it to drip in the front porch. He followed Mr Walker into the living room. Even though he had been in the room many times before, he felt now as though he was seeing it for the first time. There were comfortable armchairs, a piano, coffee tables and a large antique sideboard. A grandfather clock stood against one wall and, glancing around the room, Jake noticed that there were at least five other clocks in the room. Four large paintings hung on the walls, and other smaller ones were dotted around the room. The larger paintings depicted the scenic beauty of the African bush - vistas with plane trees, watering holes, all set against the backdrop of Mount Kilimanjaro - while the smaller ones were mainly of animals.

"I've always liked these paintings, you know," said Jake. "Somehow I like them more now that I know you painted them. They're very good."

"That's kind of you to say," said Mr Walker. "If you let me know which one you like best, perhaps I'll leave it to you after I'm gone."

"Oh, I'm sure that won't happen for years yet," said Jake, feeling slightly embarrassed. "At least, I hope it won't."

"I hope so, too," said Mr Walker. "But it's good to plan ahead and be prepared, just in case. Which is why I wanted to see you this afternoon."

"What do you mean?"

"Tell me, Jakey. Apart from the paintings, what do you find most noticeable about this room?" asked Mr Walker.

Jake looked around him again.

"Well, I've been in this room loads of times before, Mr Walker, but I can't remember seeing so many clocks before. You seem to have quite a collection."

"Indeed I do. I haven't always had so many in this room, but I've always been rather fascinated by time. But before I go on, let's have some tea."

Mr Walker went to the kitchen, and returned a couple of minutes later with a tray of tea and biscuits, which he set down on the central coffee table. He poured out two cups and handed one to Jake.

"Thanks," said Jake. "So what is it you wanted to talk to me about, Mr Walker?"

"Well, I've wanted to have a chat with you for some time, Jakey. I'm not quite sure of the best way to approach the subject but – well, it's about my other career."

"Your *other* career?" asked Jake. "I thought you said the other day that you had been an artist all your life."

"Indeed I did, and that was true. But I have another career, a rather more unusual one that I didn't mention. I am also what is known as a 'Timekeeper'," he said.

"You mean at sporting events and things like that?"

"No, not quite like that. Dear me, how do I put it?" said Mr Walker. "Ah, I know. Tell me, how many biscuits are there on that plate in front of you?"

Puzzled, Jake glanced down at the plate. "Four," he said, looking back at Mr Walker.

"How many?"

Jake looked again.

"Fo – er, three," he said. "But how...?" He looked around the table, and lifted up the plate, but there was no sign of the fourth biscuit.

"A little demonstration, my boy, of what I am about to explain. You may remember the disappearance of your peanut butter sandwich yesterday?"

Jake looked at him, incredulous.

"What – how...?" he asked.

"And the glass of milk, too."

"Yes, but... How do you know about that?" Jake's mind was racing, working overtime. But he still wasn't ready for Mr Walker's response.

"Well, I'm afraid it was me."

"You? But you weren't even there. I was alone. I only turned around for a second, and the sandwich just vanished. Same with the milk. No, you couldn't have done it, I'd have seen you, or at least heard you. I must've – "

"Jake, calm yourself" said Mr Walker. "That just goes to show that what I am about to tell you will probably be hard for you to believe. That's why I did those little demonstrations: the sandwich, the milk and the biscuit. It's not a trick, nor is it a game. In fact, it is highly secret. But before I go on, you need to promise me that you will not reveal to another living soul anything that I am about to say. Not your sister, your parents, your friends, not anybody. I know that may be a hard promise to make, but I can assure you it is necessary."

Jake's mind was buzzing. What on earth is this all about? he thought to himself. He started trying to figure out how Mr Walker could have done those things. Was he some kind of magician, a spy – or perhaps even a ghost? He hoped he looked slightly more relaxed than he felt.

Well, he thought, there's no point in me trying to figure it out, especially when he's offering to tell me anyway.

"Of course, Mr Walker," he said, trying to sound casual but sincere. "Whatever you say to me will stay between us. I promise."

"Good lad," said Mr Walker. "It's a bit of a long story, I'm afraid, but I think it'll keep your attention."

"I'm listening," said Jake.

"Excellent", said Mr Walker. He took a deep breath, and started.

"I'm a Timekeeper," he said. "To be more precise, I am one of the six Keepers of Time. Each Timekeeper is chosen personally, and holds his or her position until they wish to relinquish it to another. I am now ready to relinquish my position, and I want you to be my successor."

Mr Walker paused at this point, but Jake said nothing, feeling instinctively that he was not expected to speak. He didn't know what he would have said anyway. Silence was in fact the reaction that Mr Walker had been looking for, and he looked at Jake with something like fatherly pride.

"You don't have to decide right away, of course. I'll do my best to explain what it's all about and why I wish to choose you as my successor. If, after that, you feel you do not want to take on this responsibility, we can arrange for this conversation never to have taken place. You'll see what I mean in due course." Jake sat there, realising that he couldn't have spoken even if he'd wanted to. Mr Walker went on.

"As a Timekeeper, I am known as the Freezer. I need only to click my fingers once, and time will freeze. When this happens, everything stops precisely at that same moment – people, clocks, transport, birds, clouds, even waves on the beach. Only when I click my fingers again will time restart, exactly at the moment it stopped. It is impossible for anybody to tell when this has happened. But you know that, of course. You could not notice it when the sandwich and the biscuit vanished before your eyes and, if you think about it now, you will still be unable to recall the instant when time stopped and restarted."

Mr Walker watched Jake's face. He was listening intently, concentrating on what was being said. His features displayed a deep and mature curiosity, rather than any excitement or incredulity – which may well have been the reaction of many people twice his age.

"You've probably got a million questions you want to ask already. If it helps, I don't mind if you ask questions as we go along."

"I'm not quite sure where to start," said Jake slowly. "It's a pretty big thing to take in at this stage. I think I'd like to listen a bit longer, but I have a couple of questions now."

"Fire away."

"You said there are six Keepers of Time. Who are the others?"

"Yes, there are six of us in total. There's the Master, who has overall control. Then there's Traveller, Seeker, Retro, Splitter and myself. We all work, independently or together, for the Master. As I've said already, I'm known as Freezer, because I can freeze time. So it is with most of the others. Seeker can go forwards in time, whilst Retro can go backwards. Splitter can be in two places at once. None of the four of us can do anything that the others can do, unless our hands are joined at the time. Traveller, however, can do anything, since he is the link between us and the Master. He also convenes meetings of the Keepers, which take place whenever we wish to discuss something of importance. I have arranged a meeting this afternoon, in fact, to introduce you to them."

"It sounds fascinating. But what if I decide not to take on these responsibilities? You said something about arranging for this conversation never to have taken place?"

"That's easy," said Mr Walker. "I just ask Retro to take you back in time – perhaps to when you rang my doorbell this afternoon – and you'll never know anything about it. We will probably talk about fishing or football instead."

"Awesome," said Jake. "That can really happen?"

"Sure it can," said Mr Walker. "And our powers are used every single day, for one reason or another, but nobody ever knows. The important thing to remember is that our powers are only to be used for good reason, and never for personal gain. That rule is sacred, and any Keeper who wrongly uses his or her powers will be severely reprimanded by the Master. If there was no such rule, you can imagine the problems we would have. Seeker, for example, could go forward in time to see next week's winning lottery numbers. Retro could go back in time and retake her exams. Splitter could commit dreadful crimes whilst having a cast-iron alibi at the same time. And I could do just about anything when nobody is able to move."

"By clicking your fingers? How does it work?" asked Jake.

"That power is given to me by the Master," explained Mr Walker. "Of course, when I transfer that power, I won't have it any more. But even though I have that power now, it doesn't mean that I can explain it. I don't actually know how it works, but it does."

"So who exactly are the others?" asked Jake. "Where do they come from, and who chose them?"

"They're ordinary people, just like you and me. Except for the Master, that is. He is timeless, and ageless. He has been in charge of time since the concept was invented. And in the fifty-seven years since I've known him, he hasn't looked a day older. He always looks, to me, around seventy. But he must be thousands, if not millions, of years old. As for the rest of us, we were chosen by different people at different times. I was chosen by an old soldier who fought in the First World War. My goodness, the stories he used to tell! He used his powers countless times to save the lives of his comrades. If he saw a machine gunner taking aim, he would freeze time, and run over and nudge the gun up a little so that the first few bullets went too high. By the time the enemy had realised the aim was wrong, his comrades had been alerted and had dived for cover. And when grenades were thrown, he would grab them from the air and throw them far away in a different direction so that they exploded harmlessly. The enemy never could understand what was going on!"

"That's amazing," said Jake. "To be able to save lives by using those powers must be so rewarding. What about the others - Seeker, Retro and Splitter?"

"You'll meet them in a little while," said Mr Walker. "You can ask them yourself."

"But how do you meet them, and where?" Jake managed to restrain the thousands of other questions bursting from his lips.

"Ah, well that's the really clever bit. And it's the only time you need to use a piece of equipment." He reached into his pocket, brought out an object and handed it to Jake.

"A pocket watch," said Jake. "I suppose I might have guessed it had something to do with time. It looks old, like one of those pocket watches that Victorian gentlemen used to wear on a chain attached to their waistcoats. But it looks so….ordinary, in that sort of way."

"Of course it looks ordinary," said Mr Walker. "It wouldn't do to be seen to carry something around with you which says 'time travel equipment' printed on it. But it's actually very special. Here, I'll show you how it works. It's almost time we went, anyway."

Mr Walker took back the pocket watch, and opened it so that Jake could see the dial clearly.

"The watch is in perfect working order – as you might expect, since it belongs to a Timekeeper," said Mr Walker. "We all have the same kind of pocket watch, and they're all synchronised to exactly the same time. If you look carefully, however, you'll notice that the minute hand is actually made up of two very thin pieces of metal."

Jake took back the watch, and examined it again carefully. "So it is," he said after a few seconds. "But you need to look really closely to notice it. What does it mean?"

"Well," said Mr Walker. "To set the time on these old timepieces – not that we need to, of course – you need to lift up and turn the little gold crown on top of the watch. It's just the same as adjusting your own watch, in fact, except that the crown is put on the side of the watch nowadays since it's worn on the wrist. But if you push down on the crown of this watch, you can then move one half of the minute hand. Now, look more closely. Can you see the three red markings on the face of the watch?"

Jake peered closer.

"Yes," he said. "They looked almost like specks of dust the first time I looked at the watch. There are red dots beside the numbers two and ten, and one below the number six."

"That's right. You place half of the minute hand on the number two to contact the Traveller. You usually do this if you want to arrange a meeting, although you can contact the Traveller about anything. And placing it on the six takes you to a pre-arranged meeting with the other Timekeepers. We'll do that soon, and you can see how it works."

"And number ten?" asked Jake.

"The number ten is for use in emergencies only," said Mr Walker. "It calls all the Timekeepers to you, wherever you are. The first time I used it, to see what happened – boy, did I get a rocket from the Master! He said it was like crying wolf. Fortunately, when I did need to use it in a real emergency, my colleagues still all came at once."

"What happened?" asked Jake. "I mean, what was the emergency?"

Mr Walker looked down. It was a few seconds before he spoke and, when he did, his voice was quiet and a little shaky.

"I – I don't really want to talk about that, Jakey. I'll tell you one day, I promise, but it's a tale that is still a bit too painful for me to recount at the moment."

"I'm sorry," said Jake. "I didn't mean to upset you, Mr Walker. It really doesn't matter what you used it for. It's just one of those questions I couldn't help myself asking."

"No, no," said Mr Walker. "I want you to ask questions. As many as you can think of, please. I hope I'll be able to answer them all but, if for any reason I can't, I promise I'll let you know the answer in due course."

"Okay," said Jake. "So - why me?"

"Pardon?"

"Why do you want me to be your successor?"

"Oh, that's a simple one to answer," said Mr Walker. "I've known you all your life, Jakey. You're like the son I never had. In quite a lot of ways, you remind me of myself when I was your age, so you're a natural choice."

"You knew I'd say yes, didn't you?"

Mr Walker smiled. "I knew you'd *probably* say yes. You're bright, inquisitive, mature, and I think you've got what it takes to make a great Timekeeper. And you're young. I'm getting too old for this now – a bit of arthritis, and not as energetic as I used to be. It's time I retired, I reckon. But I'll still be here to give you any help you need. My goodness, is that the time? We should be on our way." He stood up, and Jake jumped up too.

"How do we get to.....wherever it is we're going?" asked Jake.

"All you need to do is hold my hand. You'll be perfectly safe, trust me. Time will stop the instant we go, and will restart when we come back. We may be there for some time, but it won't actually be any time at all." Mr Walker chuckled to himself. "You know, even after all these years, I still can't get used to the idea of that!"

"And how do we get back again? You said we use the number six to get there – how do we return?"

"Simple. Just reunite the two halves of the minute hand, and we'll be back as if we'd never been anywhere."

"One last question," said Jake. "What happens if I let go of your hand?"

"You'll be right back here, although you won't be able to move until I get back and restart time, of course. But getting there and back takes only a fraction of a second – you won't have time to let go. Nothing to worry about. Now, I'll just push the crown down with my left hand, and I can turn it with my thumb. Ready? Take my right hand, and we'll go."

With some trepidation, Jake took hold of Mr Walker's right hand, squeezing it a little tighter than perhaps he needed to. With his left thumb, Mr Walker pushed and turned the crown of the pocket watch. When half of the minute hand was on the number six, he released the pressure on the crown, and they vanished.

CHAPTER THREE

He had expected to feel some sort of flying sensation, but it seemed to Jake that they hadn't actually moved at all. It was as if the room around them had suddenly changed in a flash. Jake looked around him. They were in a huge square room. There were no windows, no door and no furniture. It was brightly lit, but Jake couldn't see where the light was coming from. The walls and floor were all like stainless steel, but it felt softer. There was absolute silence.

"Can I let go of your hand now?" he whispered.

"Please do," replied Mr Walker. "I'd quite like to get the blood circulating again."

"Sorry." Jake let go, half expecting something to happen, but it didn't.

"That's alright. I was pretty nervous the first time I came here as well. I remember it like yesterday. How time flies, eh?" Mr Walker smiled, and nudged Jake in the ribs.

"Yeah, funny one," said Jake. "So, where exactly are we?"

"Who knows? I certainly don't. Our meetings have always taken place in this room, but I've no idea where it is. It could be on a different planet, for all I know. But it's a very calm place, don't you think?"

Jake thought about it. "I suppose it is. Normally, I think it'd be quite frightening to find yourself in a room without windows or doors, not knowing where you are or how you got here. But, strangely, I don't feel frightened at all. What about the others?"

"Oh, they'll be here in a second. The Keeper who calls the meeting always arrives first. It's polite, after all. Once you're here, the others follow automatically."

Even though Jake was expecting it, he almost jumped out of his skin when five other people suddenly appeared in the room simultaneously. Together with Jake and Mr Walker, they formed a natural circle. One of them, who Jake presumed to be the Master, was wearing a black cloak with a large hood that covered all his features. The other four Keepers - two men and two women - looked like normal people that Jake might pass in the street any day of the week. He wasn't sure why this surprised him: after all, Mr Walker looked entirely normal, too.

"Keepers, welcome," said Mr Walker. "I'm grateful to you for coming together to meet my chosen successor as the Freezer. This is Jake." He turned to Jake. "Jakey, these are my fellow Keepers."

Jake felt all eyes turn towards him. Even though he couldn't see the Master's eyes, he was sure they were looking in his direction as well.

"H-how do you do?" stammered Jake, feeling slightly uncomfortable under the gaze of all those present.

A deep, gentle voice came from within the hooded cloak. "Welcome, Jake. Freezer has told me much about you, and I have been greatly impressed by what I have heard. Have you yet had a chance to consider whether or not you wish to accept the honour that Freezer wishes to bestow upon you?"

"Well, sir…," Jake started.

"Please, Jake, call me Master. When we come together to meet in this room, we refer to each other only by our titles. Besides, unlike the other Keepers, Master is actually my real name as well as my title. Strange, I admit. But, please, call me Master."

"Okay - Master. I'm afraid this is all still a bit new to me, and I think there's a lot that I still need to understand. I heard about the Keepers for the first time only this afternoon at Mr Wal – I mean, Freezer's – house. But I trust Freezer and, if he thinks I am ready to take on these responsibilities, then I am ready to accept that honour."

"You speak well for someone so youthful," said Master. "Freezer is a good Keeper, well trusted by his colleagues here. His judgement is that you are ready, and we accept his judgement without hesitation. Are we all agreed?"

The other four keepers nodded their assent.

"So be it. From this moment on, Jake, you shall be known among us as the Freezer. You are welcomed to this elite circle with open arms. Mr Walker, would you please pass to Freezer the Keeper's timepiece?"

Mr Walker took the pocket watch from his waistcoat, and looked lovingly at it for a few seconds. He took Jake's hand, placed the watch in his palm, and closed his fingers over it gently. Then he took a deep breath, before speaking in a calm and clear voice.

"With this Timepiece, I pass to you the guardianship of time. I hereby relinquish my duties, and my claim to the honoured and ancient title of Timekeeper." He looked back at the Master. "Master, I thank you for allowing me to serve you all these years."

"On the contrary," said the Master, "it is I who should thank you for your service of many years. Your retirement is well deserved, my friend, and I shall miss you greatly. But this is no time for sadness, this is a time for celebration. The ceremony is complete. Let me embrace you."

Mr Walker took a few paces into the middle of the circle to meet the Master, and they embraced as old friends. Jake felt extraordinarily moved, and wondered how he could ever hope to live up to Mr Walker's example as a Timekeeper. He suddenly felt the weight of responsibility settle on his shoulders, and he looked down at the pocket watch in his hand. His worry was immediately replaced by a deep sense of pride, and he put the watch carefully into his pocket. He looked up again at the two men embracing and, without knowing why, he clapped. The others started clapping too, until the two men finally parted.

"Now, Freezer," said the Master, "let me introduce you to your new colleagues."

As he spoke, the Master pushed the hood back over his head. As Mr Walker had said, he looked around seventy. The thing that struck Jake at once were his eyes. They were the brightest blue that Jake had ever seen. His grey hair was cropped short, as was his beard. The lines at the side of his mouth and eyes indicated humour and kindness, and Jake warmed to him immediately.

"This is the Traveller," he went on. "Traveller is my closest associate. He will visit you from time to time, and will always make himself available to you for advice or assistance, should you need it. I trust that Mr Walker has explained briefly to you the functions of each of the Keepers?"

"Yes, Master," replied Jake.

Traveller was a young man of around thirty, Jake thought. He wore jeans, a checked shirt, trainers and a baseball cap. He smiled and nodded at Jake, who nodded back.

"Next to Traveller is the Seeker," the Master continued.

Seeker was a middle-aged lady in a tweed skirt and white blouse. Her glasses dangled on her chest from a chain around her neck. She had shoulder-length wavy brown hair, and two thick gold bracelets adorned her wrists. She smiled warmly at Jake.

"On your right is Retro," said the Master, indicating a black girl of around twenty years old. She wore leather trousers and a colourful silk shirt. She winked at Jake, and gave a little wave with a slender hand.

"And finally we have the Splitter."

Splitter looked a real mess. He looked as though he had just got out of bed. His shirt was partly untucked, and his hair was unkempt. But he had a happy face, and did not seem to care about his appearance. He gave a 'thumbs-up' sign to Jake.

The Master came over to Jake and shook his hand.

"Once again, welcome," he said. "You have now been entrusted with the powers of a Timekeeper. There are rules governing the use of such powers, and you'll know that they should be used wisely, for the good of others. If in doubt, ask the Traveller. Or, indeed, you can ask Mr Walker. Despite no longer being a Timekeeper, he will retain the knowledge and all the memories he acquired during his many years of service. I am sure his guidance will prove invaluable to you. No other mortal is aware of our existence. There is only one other former colleague still alive, but his situation is different and we prefer not to mention him."

Jake nodded.

"Now," the Master continued in a lighter tone, "you'll no doubt want to get to know your new colleagues a little better, so I'll leave you to it. I must go anyway, but I'll see you again before long. In the meantime, you have much to learn. Listen well to what Mr Walker has to tell you."

And with that, the Master vanished. Jake doubted that he'd ever get used to people doing that.

After the Master had left, the other Keepers gathered round Jake and Mr Walker. All of them offered their congratulations to Jake, and expressed their sorrow at the retirement of Mr Walker.

"So, Jake," said the Traveller, "how do you feel now that you're a Timekeeper?"

"I haven't really had much time to think about it," said Jake. "It feels like an honour, and I'm obviously proud that Mr Walker chose me as his successor. If I'm honest, however, I'd say that I was worried about two things. Firstly, that I'm very young. And, secondly, that I won't be able to live up to everybody's expectations."

"Well, we can put your mind at rest on those points," said Seeker. "Retro and I were both around your age when we started, and Splitter was even younger – eleven, weren't you, Splitter?"

"Twelve, actually," he replied. "But I was quite advanced for my age."

The Traveller put a hand over his mouth in a stage whisper to Jake. "He still acts like a twelve-year-old most of the time." The others, including Splitter, laughed easily.

"What about you?" Jake asked the Traveller.

"Me? I was twenty seven, and that was ten years ago. I was a late starter compared to this lot. But there are huge advantages in starting young. You get the mistakes out of the way early on. You play around with your powers for a while – like a child with a new toy, I suppose – but then you put them to good use. It's like in real life. If an adult buys a new computer for the first time, he probably spends most of his time playing games on it. But a child that grows up with computers plays all the games as a child, and then learns to put the computer expertly to the use it was originally intended for."

"I know what you mean," said Jake. "My dad is always playing computer games, and they're usually the easy card games like Solitaire. He hardly ever does anything else with the computer."

"Well, I can't use a computer," said Mr Walker. "Never could get the hang of them. But we all made mistakes early on, Jake. You will, too. It's inevitable. My job now is to help you avoid some mistakes, and Traveller will do what he can to minimise their impact, if that is necessary."

"Take it from me," said Retro, "I've made my fair share of mistakes. One time, I had to go back to do the same job eighteen times before I got it right. Man, was that boring! But it's the experience that you learn from. Relax and enjoy, that's my advice."

"And on that note," said Mr Walker, "I think it's time we were getting back to reality. Jake and I have a lot to talk about."

He passed around the group, warmly hugging each one in turn. There were tears in their eyes, prompted by the silent acknowledgement that they would never meet again.

Mr Walker wiped his eyes and put his hand on Jake's shoulder.

"My friends, I bid you farewell," he said.

They bowed their heads in respect.

"Hey, Jake," said Seeker, breaking the awkward silence. "In case we don't meet soon, I just wanted to congratulate you on your exam results – brilliant stuff!"

"Stop showing off, Seeker!" said the Traveller. He winked at Jake. "But I've got to agree, Jake – well done!"

"But how do you – ?"

"We may not be allowed to use our powers for our own benefit," said the Traveller, "but it doesn't do any harm to use them for the benefit of colleagues every now and then!"

Jake smiled at him. "Thanks," he said.

"Come, Jake," said Mr Walker. "We must leave. But I'm afraid that, this time, I need to hold your hand. I don't have the power any more, do I?"

Jake couldn't wait to try it out. "Okay, let's do it. It was nice to meet you all. Thanks for being so – well, you know, welcoming."

He went over and shook hands with each of them, and then went back and stood next to Mr Walker. He took the pocket watch out of his trousers, and pushed the crown down. He held Mr Walker's hand, and turned the crown with his thumb as he had been shown earlier. As soon as the halves of the minute hand met, Jake and Mr Walker were once again standing in Mr Walker's lounge.

"I did it!" said Jake. "I did it!"

"You did indeed, Jakey," said Mr Walker. "And look at the time. It's the same time as when we left, although I'd reckon we've been gone about half an hour, wouldn't you say?"

"Incredible," said Jake. "I would never have believed it."

"Well, that's the first lesson dealt with. Now, we'll finish our tea – it's still hot, you see – and then we'll move on to lesson number two."

CHAPTER FOUR

Lesson number two was finger-clicking. Even though he knew what would happen, Jake wasn't ready for the experience of being able to stop time. The first time he clicked his fingers, everything froze. It was quite scary, really. Mr Walker was like a statue, and all the clocks stopped ticking at once. He walked to the window and looked out. A man was walking his dog along the pavement, but both were frozen to the spot. Looking up, he saw a sparrow that seemed to be hanging in mid flight, perfectly still. It was as if he had pushed the 'pause' button on a video. He clicked his fingers again, and time restarted.

"It really works!" said Jake excitedly. "This is wicked!"

"I don't know about wicked," said Mr Walker, "but that's the strangest experience I've had for almost sixty years. Time froze, and it wasn't me that did it. If it hadn't been for your basic mistake, I'd never have known."

"Mistake?" said Jake. "What mistake?"

"You moved! You must remember that time stops for everybody except you. That means that, when you restart time, you must be in exactly the same place as you were when you stopped it. If you're suddenly several feet away in the blink of an eye, it's obvious that something happened that can't be explained."

"Of course," said Jake. "I didn't think of that. How stupid of me."

"Never mind," said Mr Walker. "Nobody noticed except me. It's lucky your first attempt was made in private, rather than in the middle of town. That would have caused quite a stir. It's okay, Jakey. Remember what Retro said about mistakes? You're bound to make them early on, especially when you're not used to your new powers. You're not likely to forget that one, anyway."

"I hope not. But it might take a bit of practice to get right, I reckon."

"You'll be fine," said Mr Walker. "You can practice it......."

Jake clicked his fingers again, and Mr Walker froze in mid sentence. Jake went over to the table, finished his tea and ate one of the remaining biscuits. He still felt quite nervous, almost as if he was being watched, but he told himself not to be so silly. He counted to ten, and went back to exactly the same place that he had been standing when he had stopped time. He composed himself, and clicked his fingers.

"....as often as you like, from now on," Mr Walker finished. He showed no sign of having realised that Jake had stopped time. He looked at Jake. "What are you grinning for?"

"Looks like I've fooled the teacher on my second attempt."

"You mean – you did it again, just then?"

"Whilst you were talking. See how many biscuits there are now?"

Mr Walker looked at the plate.

"My word," he said. He looked back at Jake, feeling as if his heart would burst with pride. "Never in my wildest dreams did I think that you'd pick it up that well. That's truly astonishing. It took me ages to get that right, when I started."

"I'll still need to practice," said Jake. "I tried really hard that time, but getting it right every time is going to be more difficult than I thought."

"Well," said Mr Walker. "I think we'd better call it a day for now. You can't learn too much in one go, or you'll forget things. Why not spend a couple of days practising that first? Do it on your own to begin with, just so you can get used to it. Then maybe try it out on the family. But - however tempting it might be - no naughty tricks on your sister, right?"

"Okay."

"And one more golden rule."

"What's that?"

"Nothing to be written down," said Mr Walker. "Never record your actions, never keep a diary of what you do with your powers, or how you use them. Something in writing will always be found eventually. You must keep it all in your head. Understood?"

"Understood," said Jake. "But what about the pocket watch? What if somebody sees that, and asks questions?"

"Keep the pocket watch with you, or close to you, at all times. You can always say that I gave it to you as a gift. Well, I did in fact! But don't go showing it off. Show it to the family today, then you won't need to hide it from them. Tell them I was having a clear out of old things. And," he looked around the room for a second, "why not give this other little timepiece to Alice? It'll look far less suspicious if I've given you both something."

"Good idea," said Jake. "Thanks. I'm sure Alice will like it."

They walked slowly to the front door, which Mr Walker opened.

"Looks like it's dried up a bit. You shouldn't need your umbrella on the way home."

Jake stood there, not really knowing what to say.

"Mr Walker," he started. "I just wanted to say...." He broke off, not knowing how to finish the sentence without sounding daft.

"It's okay, Jakey. I understand what you mean. This is a big step, for both of us. Go on home. I'm always here if you need me, and you know you're welcome any time. Maybe you could drop by on the way home from school on Monday, and you can tell me how it's all going."

"I'll do that."

Mr Walker held out his hand but, on impulse, Jake gave him a hug. He hadn't done that before, but it felt like the most natural thing in the world at that moment. Mr Walker patted him on the back. Jake turned, picked up his umbrella, and walked briskly up the path and turned onto the pavement towards his own house.

Jake went to bed early that night. He was exhausted after what had been the most remarkable day of his life. And after all, he thought to himself on his way up the stairs, his day had actually been quite a bit longer than anybody else's. He put the pocket watch in the drawer of his bedside table, turned off the light, and fell asleep almost instantly.

On Sunday morning, Jake woke up early. He reached over and opened the drawer of his bedside table. The pocket watch was there, so it couldn't have all been a dream, could it? He picked it up and went quietly downstairs, and made himself some tea and toast. While he was waiting for the kettle to boil, he looked down at his hands. Did they really contain all that power? Well, there was only one way to find out. He clicked his fingers. Everything stopped. The kettle stopped boiling, the kitchen clock stopped ticking, and the birds singing outside the window fell silent. He went to the bottom of the stairs, and stood there listening carefully. Even his dad had stopped snoring. Not a sound could be heard throughout the house. He clicked his fingers again, and normal service was resumed. Nobody else was about, so it didn't matter that he wasn't in the same place as when he stopped time. Nevertheless, he would have to be careful about that. He didn't know if he felt pleased, relieved, excited or simply stunned by the realisation that he was, indeed, a Timekeeper.

He sat down and ate his toast. He was glad nobody else was awake yet. It gave him time to think.

Alice came downstairs, rubbing her eyes sleepily and yawning. She was three years younger than Jake, but she was almost as tall.

"Morning," she said.

"Hi," replied Jake.

"You're not usually up at this time on a Sunday morning."

"Couldn't sleep, so I decided to get up."

Jake felt slightly uncomfortable. He and Alice were actually good friends. They spent a lot of time talking, and he usually told her everything. But he knew that he could never tell her about being a Timekeeper. Much as he trusted her, he knew that he must never reveal the secret, and that made him feel slightly sad. It would be good to have somebody to talk to about it. Even though he was very fond of Mr Walker, it wasn't the same. Mr Walker was almost seventy years older than him: they were from different generations.

"I saw Mr Walker yesterday," said Jake. "He was having a clear-out, and gave me this pocket watch." He held it out, and Alice took it from him.

"That's nice," she said, turning it over in her hand. "It looks quite old. You can't do much with it, though. You can't wear it on your wrist, and you don't wear a waistcoat."

"No, but I really like it all the same. He's had it for years. Apparently he got it from a soldier after the First World War." At least, Jake thought, I can tell her some of the truth. "Here, he asked me to give you this clock." He passed her a small mantle clock, which had a plain white face with roman numerals. The timepiece was set into sparkling glass crystal.

"Oh, it's beautiful," said Alice. "It'll look really nice on my dressing table. I'll have to go over and thank him later."

Sunday passed quietly, as usual. Jake's mum had a mountain of washing and ironing to do, while his dad played in a golf competition at the local club. Alice spent most of the day on the telephone to her friends, or listening to music in her room. Jake, of course, had to tidy his bedroom, which took up most of the morning. When he was finished, he wandered off to the copse of trees for an hour or so, and sat there thinking. He clicked his fingers a few times, trying to get used to his new power, but he realised it was pretty pointless in the copse. Not a lot moved there when time was running, so it was difficult to see a difference.

He returned to the house, and continued to experiment. He would stop time, walk around and make noises. There was no reaction from his mother or his sister. He would carefully reposition himself before restarting time again. He did this several times until he felt more confident about it. Eventually, he decided to stop practising, and did some revision for his exams. Even though Seeker and the Traveller had said he would do well, he didn't think he should ignore his studies completely. He concentrated hard for a few hours until supper time – always a roast on Sunday – and spent the rest of the evening in front of the television. By nine o'clock, he'd had enough of the mindless programmes which seemed to be repeated so often, so he went upstairs and once again collapsed into bed. Just before he fell asleep, he resisted the temptation to click his fingers just one more time. If he did that and forgot to click again, he'd wake up perfectly refreshed to find that it was still only Sunday evening! Then he'd be awake all night, and he'd be exhausted before he even got to school.

CHAPTER FIVE

On Monday morning, he felt ready to face the world again. He put on his school clothes, placing the pocket watch carefully in the inside zip pocket of his blazer. He thought about leaving it at home, just in case it got stolen or damaged at school, but dismissed the idea. What was the point of being a Timekeeper if you leave the vital piece of equipment at home? No, he'd need to carry it with him at all times, but he'd just have to make sure that it was safe from harm. He'd have to be especially careful when Snooge was about.

Jake went downstairs for breakfast. Alice was already there, hogging the toaster as usual, so Jake contented himself with a bowl of cereal instead. As soon as he finished, he picked up his school bag and set off. It was a warm day, and he didn't want to have to arrive at school all sweaty. He could walk the distance in twenty minutes, but he allowed himself thirty this morning.

How daft to be worried about being late, he thought to himself. He could click his fingers and take ages to walk to school if he felt like it. He'd just have to go into the boys' toilets to restart time: that way, nobody would know how long he'd been there, so they could not remark that they hadn't seen him arrive. Still, *not to be used for personal benefit*, he reminded himself. Gosh, he'd have to watch that temptation closely.

The route to school was quite pleasant, especially on a sunny day. Out of Duckworth Close, over the main road, cut through the park, along the high street, past the train station, and there you were at the school gates. If it was raining, or if he was feeling lazy, there was a bus stop on the main road just near Duckworth Close, but Jake liked to browse the shops in the high street or enjoy the tranquillity of the park, so he rarely used the bus. Alice, on the other hand, hated walking, and usually rushed out of the house at the last minute in time to catch the bus. Besides, it was so totally uncool for any brother and sister to be seen walking to school together, however well they got on at home.

The school day was passing slowly. Jake realised after the first few lessons that, despite the heat, he was the only boy in his class who hadn't removed his blazer. He took it off and hung it on the back of his chair, but he didn't feel comfortable with Snooge only a few feet away. It was highly likely that Snooge would have a go at picking his pockets to see if

31

there was any money to be found. Jake wanted to transfer the pocket watch to his trouser pocket, but that would certainly arouse Snooge's interest if he spotted it.

But I don't need to take that risk, he thought.

Click!

Everything froze. The teacher stopped talking in mid sentence, his arm outstretched as he wrote a mathematical formula on the whiteboard.

Jake looked around the class. As he had now come to expect, everybody sat there with a frozen expression. Jake transferred the pocket watch from his blazer to his trousers, and repositioned himself ready to start time again. He resisted the urge to tie Snooge's shoe laces together, just for the fun of it.

Click!

Back to normality. A glance around the room confirmed that none of his fellow students showed any signs of knowing that time had briefly stopped. But Snooge caught his eye as he looked in his direction, and gave a little snarl. Damn, thought Jake, I shouldn't have worried about checking. He'll be after me now, just for looking at him.

And he was. Snooge approached Jake within seconds of getting outside during break. He grabbed Jake's arm.

"Yeah, what were you looking at in there, Hepton?"

"Ouch – get off, Snooge, you're hurting."

"Really? Well, it costs a quid, remember? Oh, and another quid for looking at me. Pay up, Hepton, or you'll get more of this later."

"Alright, alright," said Jake.

He pulled the money from his pocket, and handed it over. Snooge put the coins in his own pocket, and released Jake's arm.

"Great doing business with you, as usual!" Snooge chuckled as he ambled off, leaving Jake rubbing his arm.

Snooge was several yards away by now, with his back to Jake. Yeah? muttered Jake to himself. Let's see what you make of this, then.

Click!

Everything stopped. Jake carefully checked his position before moving. He'd have to be very careful, since there were loads of people around. He walked up to Snooge, and round to his front, where he saw that his features were frozen in a malevolent grin. Carefully, he reached into Snooge's pocket and retrieved his money, then returned to his original spot and took time to compose himself.

Click!

The activity and noise of the school playground resumed instantly. Snooge continued on his way, unaware that anything had happened.

"Hey, Jake," said a voice.

Jake's heart missed a beat. One of his friends, George White, was approaching him. Oh no, Jake thought. Had George seen something? He cursed himself for being so stupid. He shouldn't have bothered taking such a risk with so many people about. He held his breath as George reached him.

"I saw Snooge got you again," said George. "You okay?"

Jake let out a sigh of relief, although George took it as a sign of resignation that he'd lost his lunch money again.

"Yeah, I'm fine. It's no big deal," he replied.

"Want to borrow some cash for lunch? I've got some spare," said George.

"What? Er, no thanks. Cheers, George, but I've still got some cash. Snooge wasn't quite as successful as he thought he'd been."

"Fine," said George. "You know, I was just talking to Adam and Giles. We're planning a revenge strike on Snooge in the next couple of days. Interested?"

"Sure, count me in," said Jake. "It's about time we put a stop to Snooge's antics once and for all. In fact, I think I've made a start already."

"What do you mean?" asked George.

"Eh? Oh, never mind. Let's make a plan together. He can't take all four of us on," said Jake.

After double maths, Jake joined George, Adam and Giles in the lunch queue. The school canteen was already half full, and the queue was long. They were just beginning to talk about how to exact suitable revenge on Snooge when they heard a commotion further up the line.

Snooge stood at the cash till, with a tray full of food in front of him. He was searching his pockets, turning them inside out.

"I had the money in here earlier," he said in a loud voice. "Somebody must've stolen it off me."

"Oh, sure," said the dinner lady at the cash till. "And who'd be stupid enough to steal money from Patrick Snooge? Besides, if it had been in your trouser pocket, you'd have felt someone trying to steal it."

"I'm telling you, I had the money on me earlier," said Snooge, now red with anger and embarrassment. The volume of noise in the canteen had reduced dramatically when the other pupils saw what was going on. Everybody was looking at Snooge, many of them with satisfied grins.

"Well, if you don't have it on you now, you don't have lunch," said the dinner lady.

"What? But I'm hungry! I always have a big lunch," argued Snooge. "Look, I'll give it to you tomorrow, okay?"

The dinner lady held firm. She knew Snooge's reputation.

"No chance, sonny. Pay now, or leave with nothing."

"But that's unfair! Somebody's stolen it, I tell you."

"Yeah, I've heard that from lots of pupils here," said the dinner lady, staring accusingly at Snooge. "It's amazing how much theft there is in this school."

Snooge turned to the boy standing behind him in the queue, and whispered menacingly in his ear. "Give me two quid now, or I'll flush your head down the toilet every day for a week."

The boy looked scared. He looked at the dinner lady, then around the canteen. All eyes were now on him, but that seemed to give him strength.

"No," he said in a loud voice.

A spontaneous cheer went up.

"What?" hissed Snooge. "Didn't you hear what I said I'd do?"

The boy hesitated. "I don't care," he said. "You're not having my dinner money."

The dinner lady came to his aid. "Right, Snooge, off you go. No money, no food."

Several pupils sitting at the canteen tables began slowly to thump the tables with their knives. The rhythm caught on, and Snooge looked around the canteen defiantly.

Jake saw his chance for sweet revenge.

Click!

There was sudden silence as the whole canteen came to an abrupt standstill around him. Jake knew he was pushing the boundaries of being a Timekeeper but, he told himself, this is for the good of the school rather than for personal gain.

He went up to Snooge, who was frozen to the spot holding his tray of food, and carefully undid the belt and button on his trousers. Then he returned to his original place in the queue with George, Adam and Giles. He composed himself carefully, although he could see that all eyes seemed to be fixed firmly on Snooge. It was unlikely that anybody would notice Jake if he did not recompose himself perfectly.

Click!

The commotion resumed and, in the same instant, Jake watched as Snooge's trousers fell to the floor around his feet, revealing a pair of boxer shorts with large red dots. There was a second of silence. Snooge's face turned puce as he realised what had happened. He quickly turned to put down his food tray as the canteen erupted in raucous, mocking laughter. He pulled up his trousers and tightened the belt as quickly as he could, his face showing an intriguing mixture of fury, incomprehension and deep humiliation. Then he turned, shoved the boy hard on the shoulder and stormed off. Another cheer went up, and the jeers rang in Snooge's ears as he ran down the hall from the canteen.

Several pupils went up to the boy at the front of the queue and clapped him on the back, obviously thinking that he must have had something to do with what had happened, even though he had been holding his own tray all the time. After a few moments, the boy grinned sheepishly.

The dinner lady gestured for him to come closer so that she could be heard above the noise.

"No charge for you today, son," she said. "I reckon you've earned a free lunch, eh?"

The boy grinned widely, and went off to join a table of girls who, by the welcome they gave him, appeared to be his new fan club.

Jake looked at George, Adam and Giles.

"Well," he said, "perhaps we don't need to make a plan after all. I can't see Snooge giving us any more trouble after that."

"Yeah," said George. "But I wonder who on earth was brave enough, or stupid enough, to pick Snooge's pocket – and what a time for his trousers to fall down!"

"We'll probably never know who picked his pocket," said Adam. "But whoever it was, they've done the school a huge favour."

Jake felt like shouting "it was me!", but knew that he would never be able to explain what had happened. So, still grinning from the spectacle, he nodded his silent agreement and started thinking about what he'd have for lunch.

CHAPTER SIX

Later that day, after getting home from school, Jake went to see Mr Walker as he had promised.

"Jakey," he said with a broad smile. "I was just thinking about you. How are you getting on?"

"Fine, fine," said Jake. "I wanted to let you know what happened today, but I've also got some more questions I'd like to ask, if that's okay."

"Sure it is. Tell me all about it, and ask anything you like."

Jake told him about Snooge, and what had happened in the canteen.

"The thing is," said Jake at the end, "was it wrong to use my powers for something like that? Will I get in trouble with the Master?"

Mr Walker let out a chuckle.

"Oh, I doubt it," he said. "It sounds as though Snooge is a thoroughly obnoxious boy, and I'm sure he deserved what he got. Let's hope it teaches him a lesson. If it does, then I can't see any reason why the Master should disapprove – you'll have done some good, after all. It was partly for your own satisfaction, of course, but school will definitely be a better place if Snooge changes his ways."

Jake was relieved. He didn't want to break the rules so early on in his career, and Mr Walker's reassurance eased his concerns.

"Besides," Mr Walker continued, "if you ask any of your Timekeeper colleagues how they used their powers on their first few days, you'll hear some stories that make yours pale into insignificance. You mustn't worry about it – and, if you do cross the line at all, I can assure you that you'd find the Master most accommodating of minor transgressions. Remember, he's seen hundreds, even thousands, of new Timekeepers over the years, and it's entirely human to want to try out such special powers in different ways, even if it's not always in the interests of the wider community. No, if you had done something wrong, it's likely that the Traveller would have appeared in a flash to let you know."

"That's good to know," said Jake. "Of course it's tempting to use the powers wrongly – it's like being able to do really good magic tricks, but I know that it wouldn't be wise to draw attention to myself in that way."

"That's right. It *is* magic, in a way. The difference is that magic can always be explained, if not always understood. But once a magic trick is explained, it doesn't necessarily mean that it could be done by anyone.

The magician still has special skills that sets him apart from the rest of us. Being a Timekeeper is different. We can't explain it. It's simply beyond our human comprehension. That's why the secrecy of the Timekeepers is so vital: it would be a disaster if people realised that such powers existed. You can imagine – scientists would want to find out how such powers work, others would want to use and abuse the powers, and that would endanger the very lives of the Timekeepers. Any lapse in security must be addressed instantly – Retro and Traveller have often been called on to do that – so that the work of the Timekeepers remains hidden from the world."

"That all makes sense," said Jake. "Gosh, it just brings it home to me how important it is to be responsible."

"Responsible, yes, but don't always be so serious about it. You're a naturally responsible lad, which is partly what appealed to the Master in his decision to adopt you as Freezer. Just try to remember that, if you even suspect a security lapse, do please tell Traveller. At least he can investigate it, and make sure nothing is wrong. The consequences of being identified as a Timekeeper would be infinitely worse, for everybody."

"I suppose it helps security that all the Timekeepers look so…well, ordinary," said Jake.

"Indeed. Timekeepers don't need to be experts in martial arts, and they don't need to fly. In a way, that's a shame, of course – wouldn't that be fun? But looking ordinary is a definite bonus. Timekeepers are not superheroes, although they are blessed with certain powers that enable them to do similar things. In the past, they have stopped wars and saved many, many lives in countless different ways."

"But we read all the time about children dying from disease or poverty. Why can't we do anything to stop that?"

"Ah," said Mr Walker. He put his finger lightly on his lips, thinking about the best way to answer. "You've stumbled upon one of the golden rules of being a Timekeeper. Frustrating as it may be, Timekeepers are not allowed to interfere with the *natural* course of events, nor indeed of the course of nature."

"How do you mean?" asked Jake.

"Well, let's say Seeker foresaw a major natural disaster happening. An earthquake, a flood or a volcanic eruption, for example. We can't stop those things happening, because they are going to happen anyway. Can we warn people? Well, we can but, unfortunately, few people believe a person who says they have seen the future. You know the type of person – '*The end of the world is nigh*' and all that. So Timekeepers try to warn people in an urgent, but low-key, way. Placing an anonymous article in a local newspaper, for example. But it's a sad fact – and no doubt one that I bet you agreed with until last Saturday – that most people simply don't believe that the future can be foreseen."

"You're right," said Jake.

"And what can we do about evil dictators who live in luxury at the expense of the lives of the people they are meant to govern? Time will ultimately be their judge, and perhaps they will be brought to justice, but Timekeepers can't make that happen any quicker."

"The natural course of events. Yes, I see."

"One thing I learnt early in life is that you should never underestimate the forces of nature. Nature will always win, because Nature is just about the only thing on the planet over which the human race – which includes Timekeepers – has no control."

Mr Walker paused briefly to let that sink in. "Now, you said you had some questions for me. Let me make some tea first, and then you can fire away."

"First off," said Jake, "I need to understand how to organise meetings with the others. And how do they contact me if a meeting is called?"

"That's one of Traveller's principal functions," explained Mr Walker. "He'll visit all the Timekeepers – it doesn't matter where you are or what you're doing at the time – and advise you of any meeting. The instant he appears, time stops, so only you will know that he's been and gone. It's sometimes a bit of a shock, but it's the only way to do it. If necessary, he can help you reposition yourself if you were in the middle of something."

"So how often does that happen?" he asked.

"Oh, there's no telling," said Mr Walker. "It could be once a week, or once a month. It depends on what's going on, who's called the meeting and for what purpose. Traveller will tell you all that when he visits, so you'll never arrive at a pre-arranged meeting unprepared."

"But I thought I could call all the Timekeepers together in an emergency?"

"Yes, that's the only exception. If a Timekeeper calls an emergency meeting, everybody is instantly collected and taken to wherever their colleague is. Time stops for everyone else of course, and only restarts when all the Timekeepers have returned to their original positions."

"Let's hope I'm not in the shower, then!"

"Precisely. I found out the hard way that pyjamas should always be worn in bed, if you know what I mean. A most embarrassing episode, that one!"

Jake tried to put the picture out of his mind, and vowed silently always to wear pyjamas and to have quick showers, just in case.

It was beginning to make sense, although trying to understand just how the entire system worked was fairly pointless. Nobody would ever be able to understand it properly. At least Jake was able to discuss it with somebody who had so much experience to offer. What on earth would he do when Mr Walker was no longer around?

Another question sprang to Jake's mind.

"The Master said that there was only one other former colleague still alive, but that his situation was different. What did he mean?"

"Fergus Dingley," said Mr Walker. His face exhibited a rather pained expression.

"Oh, sorry," said Jake, recalling the last time he'd seen that look on Mr Walker's face. "I didn't mean to pry."

"No, no, that's quite alright. The Timekeepers rarely talk about him, but it's important that you should know about Fergus."

Mr Walker paused for a moment before continuing.

"Fergus Dingley was Seeker's predecessor, and held the position for several years. He and I became firm friends. He lives not far from here, and we used to visit each other quite regularly. He may be only half my age, but we're both single, and both interested in art. Having spent so many years being unable to talk to anybody else about the Timekeepers, I was delighted to have a colleague who I could also call a regular friend.

"But then things went horribly wrong. Fergus had always been keen on horse racing, and enjoyed placing small bets every week. I suppose we should have seen it coming, but he had a run of bad luck and lost a fair amount of money. I suppose it was inevitable that he would attempt to use his power for personal gain. He would find out which horse had won a race, and then bet on it. He tried to cover his tracks but, once he found out how easy it was, the temptation was obviously unbearable for him. He changed noticeably.

"I discussed the matter with the Traveller, and expressed concern that Fergus might be doing something wrong. Traveller kept a close eye on his activities, and found that Fergus was in serious breach of his oath as a Timekeeper. An emergency meeting was called, and the Master had no choice but to strip Fergus of his power. He could not allow Fergus to continue as Seeker. Nor could he allow him to retain his knowledge, since he felt sure that Fergus would seek some form of retribution. So the Traveller and Retro took Fergus back to the time before his inauguration as Seeker, and left him to live his life as if nothing had ever happened. But before he went, Fergus told me that he knew that I must have been the one to tip off the Traveller, and he told me that he would never forgive me."

"It's a sad story," said Jake, "but why is it still an issue? Presumably Fergus doesn't know anything about the Timekeepers now, so he won't know that he blamed you for getting him stripped of his power."

"Yes, that should have been the case. Fergus' life took a different track after he was taken back in time, and he became a journalist. Sure, he didn't have any recollection of being a Timekeeper, and knew nothing of our existence. What we didn't know, however, was that Fergus had given himself some kind of insurance in case his betting addiction came to light. He had gone into the future and recorded my name and address, describing me as a Timekeeper. Fortunately, he didn't record details of the others, or even the fact that he was a Timekeeper himself – perhaps he thought he'd remember that. But he also recorded a few examples of what our powers had been used for.

"We hadn't suspected anything, until an article appeared in a newspaper a few years ago. It turned out that Fergus had stumbled upon the message which he had left himself about the Timekeepers. Of course, he didn't know that it was true, since he had no recollection of being Seeker. But it was written in his handwriting, and he couldn't remember writing it, so he went in search of any corroboration. He came to see me, since my name and address had been recorded. The first time he turned up, it was a real shock. There he was, a good friend of mine who I'd seen only a few years earlier. But as far as he was concerned, we'd never met! The puzzle was clearly eating away at him: why would he have recorded my name and address without knowing me or remembering why? He wouldn't let it drop, and kept asking probing questions.

"Of course, as soon as I opened the front door and saw him standing there, I froze time and contacted Traveller immediately. We agreed that I should simply be polite, but maintain that I knew nothing of what he was talking about. That would probably have been alright, but he must have seen some expression of surprise in my face the instant I opened the door to him, so he started accusing me of covering something up.

"Goodness, what a mess it was. In the end, I had to take out a restraining order against him, forbidding him to contact me. Fortunately, the authorities never believed his tale about the Timekeepers – after all, who would? – and Fergus was discredited as a journalist. But he still hasn't given up. He writes things from time to time, although he is careful not to refer to me by name. So all we can do is keep a close eye on him, and never drop our guard. As I said, it's important that you know this now, just in case, but there really should be no need for you to be concerned about it."

Jake was silent for a moment.

"Well, thanks for letting me know the whole story. It's just such a shame that you had to lose a good friend like that, and it must have been really difficult to meet him again in those circumstances."

"Perhaps the hardest thing I've ever had to do," agreed Mr Walker. "I've never had to act to cover up my role – acting isn't necessary if you can freeze time. I just didn't mention the Timekeepers to anyone, so nobody could ever be suspicious of me. But dealing with Fergus was a very stressful experience. I hope it's now firmly in the past but, as I said, he still writes things from time to time, and we need to remain cautious."

Jake needn't have worried too much about his new role over the next few weeks. Mr Walker was always there to offer advice, and usually a glass of lemonade, when Jake felt he needed it. Mr Walker was like his best friend, and the secret of the Timekeepers had made the bond between the two of them unbreakable.

Jake never tired of listening to Mr Walker's stories from his days as a Timekeeper, and Mr Walker never tired of telling them. After all, he had never been able to tell another living soul, so he was delighted to recount his adventures for Jake.

There were many stories from his time in Africa. He had used his powers to save lives – he stopped a friend of his being trampled by an elephant, and he had made sure that several traffic accidents had been averted.

Once, with Retro, he had saved a boat full of tourists from certain death when their boat hit a rock during a river cruise. The boat was sinking fast, and those tourists who managed to escape the waiting, hungry crocodiles would doubtless have perished in the fast flowing currents. He had summoned the Traveller and Retro, and discussed what should be done. They agreed that time reversal was the best course of action, so Retro took the boat back to the time when its passengers were enjoying "sundowner" drinks on the upper deck, and Mr Walker then turned the wheel of the boat to avoid the unseen rock.

On one occasion he'd been painting alone in the bush – which he knew perfectly well was not a sensible thing to do – when he had heard a noise behind him. He had looked round to stare into the yellow, demonic eyes of a lion, its teeth bared in a determined snarl of hatred. The lion had suddenly lunged forward with incredible speed, and Mr Walker had only just had time to click his fingers. The enormous beast had frozen in mid stride, just feet from its intended prey. Mr Walker had climbed as high as he could into the branches of a nearby tree before he had clicked again. The lion had stopped dead in its tracks, on the exact spot where Mr Walker would have been. The animal had seen its victim disappear into thin air, and it looked around wildly. Mr Walker watched as, with a swipe of its great front paw, the animal destroyed the easel as if it was made of matchwood. It started pacing the area, but could not understand what had happened, so had skulked off back into the bush. Mr Walker had of course abused the 'personal benefit' rule, but it had, after all, been to save his own life, and he could hardly have been criticised for that. Nevertheless it was fortunate that nobody else had been in the vicinity to witness what had happened, since he would not have been able to explain it. He would have had to choose some other course of action, but that could have been far more dangerous.

It was inevitable that, eventually, Jake's mother would notice that Jake was now spending far more time at Mr Walker's house than before, and she asked him about it. Jake had to think quickly.

"Mr Walker's helping me with my revision for the exams," he said. "I hadn't realised he knew so much about history and stuff, but it's been really useful."

"That's good, then," she said. "Your father and I aren't much help with history – I never was any good at it. But don't neglect your other subjects, will you?"

"It's alright. I reckon I'm okay on most of them," said Jake.

CHAPTER SEVEN

Jake was enjoying being a Timekeeper. After a few weeks, he was confident about using his new skills in public, having practised regularly in the High Street on the way to or from school. The first time he did this in the High Street, it had been a mistake. He had been walking to school, listening to his portable CD player, when he clicked his fingers in time to the music. Fortunately, he only clicked once before he realised, and there hadn't been many people around, but he'd still taken a few steps from where he'd been. He had to guess the position from which to restart time. Since then, he hadn't made a similar mistake

He also knew that his true role as a Timekeeper had not yet been tested properly. Apart from that Monday at school, when he had succeeded in humiliating Snooge in front of the entire canteen, he had not used his power other than for the purpose of practice. He still chuckled to himself at the memory of that. Snooge had taken the Tuesday off – unwell, according to his mother – and had returned on the Wednesday to face all the jokes and jeers of the other pupils, many of whom had previously been his victims. Since then, he had been no trouble at all. At times, Jake had even felt sorry for him, but then remembered just how much misery Snooge had previously inflicted on others before he got his comeuppance.

The school holidays had started. Most of his friends had gone on holiday, to various exotic destinations, with their families. The Heptons preferred to take their family holiday later in August: it was slightly quieter than the end of July, when it seemed the rest of the country disappeared on holiday just after the end of term. Going later in August also meant that Jake would have his exam results by then. Although he wasn't particularly worried about them, it would still be nice to relax on holiday without thinking about the dreaded envelope that would land on the doormat soon afterwards.

The High Street was fairly quiet for a Saturday morning. The weather was reasonably warm, but overcast. It hadn't changed for the last few days, but at least it hadn't rained. Jake and Alice had gone to the High Street to take back the previous night's DVD rental, after which they would browse the music shop. They both liked the fact that the absence of school uniform made it possible for them to walk together, rather than ignore each other.

All of a sudden, they heard a commotion nearby.

"Stop! Oh, help! Help!"

Jake and Alice looked across the road to where the alarm had been raised. An elderly lady was standing by her pull-along shopping trolley, her armed raised in obvious distress. The cause was not immediately clear.

"Thief! Help!" she shouted. "Somebody stop that thief."

Jake looked further along the High Street, and saw a youth running as fast as he could, clutching what appeared to be a handbag. The hooded tracksuit top made it impossible to see any features of the youth – the age, race, even the sex was hidden from view, although Jake presumed it was male: he had never seen a girl run like that.

Click!

It had been more of a reflex action than a conscious decision to do something. But, now that the world had come to a standstill, Jake found that he could decide calmly what to do to help.

The youth was almost at the end of the High Street, and would disappear into the park in a few more strides. He was frozen in mid air, his face half turned as if he was about to look behind him in case he was being chased.

What to do?, thought Jake. How do I help, but make it look like I've done nothing?

An idea started to form in his mind.

He walked up to the youth, and gently prised open the fingers of the hand holding the bag. Then he swivelled the youth ever so slightly – which was easy, since he was suspended in mid air – so that his course was almost imperceptibly changed. He checked his work, and decided that it would probably work. If it didn't, he told himself, he could always stop time again and do something different.

He trotted back to where Alice stood, her hand against her mouth in alarm as she realised what had happened. He repositioned himself next to her carefully.

Click!

"Oh, Jake," Alice said as she gripped his arm. Jake feigned alarm, but watched his plan unfold.

The youth dropped the handbag as he looked over his shoulder. He was still running at full speed when he looked down at his hand in surprise and, in doing that, he had no chance to realise that his direction had altered.

He hit the lamp post hard. The metallic *'thung'* was clearly audible even from the distance at which Jake and Alice stood. It sounded very painful. The youth stood against the lamp post for a second, and then fell straight backwards, quite unconscious. The handbag lay on the ground several metres behind him.

The "accident" had been witnessed by just about everybody in the High Street. They had all turned their attention to the sprinting figure just a second or so before he had connected with the lamp post, and most were still staring at his now-prone form.

Jake ran over and retrieved the bag, and then trotted back to the elderly lady. She seemed frozen to the spot, and Jake had to look around to check that he had not clicked his fingers by mistake. No, everything else was moving – apart from the youth, of course. Several of the shoppers had gone over to see how badly he had hurt himself. One of them was talking on a mobile phone, probably calling for the police and an ambulance.

The lady's arm was still raised, but her face displayed more amazement than fear or alarm.

"This must be yours," said Jake.

"What? Oh, er, yes," she stammered. "But what – how – he just ran straight into a lamp post, didn't he?"

"Looks like it," said Jake. "He'll have a bit of a headache when he wakes up, I reckon."

The lady found her composure at last. She put her arm down, and straightened her back.

"Good," she said sternly. "I hope it bloody well hurts. That'll teach him a lesson."

She took her bag from Jake and turned in the opposite direction, pulling her trolley along behind her. After a few yards, she stopped and turned to Jake.

"I'm sorry, young man, I didn't say thank you for retrieving my bag for me."

"Oh, that's alright," said Jake. "I hope nothing's missing, although I don't think he had time to even open it before he dropped it."

"Well, thanks all the same. Excuse my bad manners. Must've been the shock of it all."

She turned and strode purposefully off, not even glancing back to see if her assailant was alright. She needed a coffee, she decided, and perhaps just a few drops from the hip flask in her shopping trolley.

The police car drew up next to the small group who had gathered around the youth. The policeman got out of the car, put on his hat, and spoke briefly into his radio. The youth was still lying on the ground, but was struggling to sit up. He was looking groggily around, and mumbling something to himself. The small group parted as the policeman approached, and the sirens of an ambulance could be heard drawing closer.

"What happened here, then?" asked the policeman as he knelt next to the youth. "Hey, that's a nasty crack you've got on your forehead."

One of the group explained what she had seen. "We heard a shout from over the road," she said. "We didn't see him snatch the old lady's bag, but he must've done. I saw him running like the wind, but then he dropped the bag and ran straight into the lamp post."

"N-no," said the youth, holding his hand to his head. "The lamp post 'it me. It just jumped out an' 'it me. Ow!"

"The lamp post hit you?" the policeman repeated. "My, I think we'd better get that head of yours seen to pretty quickly!"

"It 'it me, I tell ya," he shouted, and then slumped backwards. "Ooh, me 'ead 'urts! You lot must've seen it, dint'ya? You, you must've – it 'it me."

"Come along, son," the policeman interrupted. "The ambulance is here now. Let's get you looked at, and then we'll go and have a chat down at the station, eh?"

While the ambulance crew was attending to the youth, the policeman spoke to several of the onlookers.

"Did any of you see that young man snatch the handbag?" He looked around. "Come to that, where *is* the handbag, and who was it snatched from?"

Jake decided to step forward.

"Excuse me, officer. The handbag belonged to a little old lady with one of those little shopping bags on wheels. I didn't see him grab the bag but, after he'd dropped it, I picked it up and gave it back to the lady."

"So where is she now?"

"I don't know. She walked off towards the post office, a couple of minutes before you got here."

"Did she say anything before she went?" the policeman asked.

"She only said something like 'I hope it bloody well hurt' when she saw that guy on the ground," said Jake.

"Okay," said the policeman, closing his notebook. "Shopping bag on wheels, you say? Small old lady, about seventy, you think?"

"I s'pose," said Jake. "She was wearing a pretty thick coat, almost like it's cold."

"A-ha. Yes, it sounds just like Mrs Phippet. We know her quite well, so I'll go round and see her later. Looks like she got her wish about that guy's head hurting, at any rate," he said, looking back at the youth. He turned round to address the group. "Right, folks, there's nothing more to see here, so on your way please. Come on, move along now please."

Obediently, the group started to disperse quietly. The ambulance crew nodded to the policeman, and he went over and spoke to them. The would-be thief needed to be checked over at the hospital, just to be on the safe side. As they loaded him into the ambulance, Jake could hear him carrying on about the lamp post.

"Yeah, I nicked her bag, awright? But I don' run into bleedin' lamp posts for the fun of it, do I? It moved, I tell ya, it bleedin' moved!"

The ambulance doors closed on his protestations and the vehicle set off at a sedate pace, with the police car following.

"Jake!"

Jake looked around and saw Traveller by his side. It was a shock. The rest of the world had come to an abrupt standstill, but Jake hadn't been responsible.

"Traveller! Where did you come from?"

The Traveller looked slightly puzzled. "I don't normally get asked that question, but I came from my garden, actually," he replied.

"Oh – er – sorry, I haven't done something wrong, have I?" asked Jake.

"What?"

"It's just that Mr Walker said that you might suddenly pop up if I did something wrong."

"Ah," said Traveller. "Well, yes, I might. But I might also suddenly 'pop up', as you put it, to congratulate you."

"Oh."

"Well done, Jake. Good job – a small one, but a good one."

"Thanks. But how did you know about it?"

"Because you stopped time, of course! Every time you freeze time, I know about it, just like I know when the others do something too. So I saw what you were doing, and thought I'd drop by and tell you it was a good piece of work."

"So you know every time I click my fingers?" asked Jake.

"Of course," said Traveller. "I tell you, it was a real pain when you first became Freezer. Clicking all day, you were, doing all that practice. And there I was, trying to get some sleep!"

"Gosh, sorry about that. I suppose I disturbed all the others as well."

"No, only me," said Traveller.

"How come? I thought all the Timekeepers would be immune."

"They are, but only when you're in physical contact with them when you click your fingers. Otherwise they freeze just like everyone else. Not me, though. I wouldn't be much use to the Master if I couldn't see what all the Timekeepers were doing, would I?"

"Yeah, of course," said Jake. "Hey, it seems like I'm still learning something every day."

"And so you should, young man. It's a big thing to take in. Even I still have things to learn."

"You?"

"Sure. Each time something happens, there's something to learn. Timekeepers use their powers for such a variety of purposes, I never stop learning. Anyway, enough of this chat. I gotta go. Better reposition yourself before I do."

Jake tried to remember how he was standing, but it was more difficult than usual.

"No, head up a little bit more, and eyes front," said Traveller. "Yeah, that's about it. Stay like that. Ready?"

"Yes," muttered Jake, trying to hold the position.

"Okay. See you soon, Freezer."

Out of the corner of his eye, Jake saw the Traveller disappear, at exactly the same instant as everything else started moving again.

"Bye," said Jake.

"Buy what?" said Alice, dragging Jake back to reality.

"What? Oh, I was just thinking about buying a drink. Fancy a coke?"

"Why not? Well, that's the excitement in this High Street over for another year! Come on, let's go."

CHAPTER EIGHT

Jake turned the envelope over and over in his hands. He'd leapt out of bed as soon as he'd heard the *snap* of the letter box and the *flump* of letters as they hit the doormat. He was the first one downstairs, although he'd heard his dad moving about getting ready for work.

Oh, well, he thought, I might as well open it.

The pulled the sheet of paper from the envelope and stared at it. Straight A's.

His first reaction was relief. Even though he'd been fairly confident, he knew that there could have been a couple of subjects in which he hadn't done so well. Then he remembered Seeker congratulating him, and he smiled to himself. He'd been scared of believing her, just in case it was all a fantasy, but it looked like she really had seen his results.

He ran upstairs and banged loudly on the bedroom doors, shouting his news. His mum and dad both came out with huge grins and gave him a hug. Even Alice emerged, yawning and still half asleep, and gave him an unexpected congratulatory kiss on the cheek.

Breakfast was longer than usual. Jake's mum did a fry-up, which normally only happened on a weekend. They discussed their holiday plans — they would be leaving in three days for a beach holiday in Majorca — and worked out all the things they needed to buy. It was decided that Jake and Alice would go shopping with their mum that morning: they should be able to get everything they needed in the High Street.

Jake was still in a bit of a daze as they walked through the park towards the High Street. His mum and Alice soon got tired of telling him to keep up, and let him drag behind in his own silent world of self-satisfied contemplation. He caught up at regular intervals anyway, thanks to their inexhaustible ability to window-shop.

Up ahead, Jake saw them cross the road, obviously heading for the chemists where they would no doubt spend a great deal of both time and money. A large sign in the window of the shop announced that there were special offers on sun cream, mosquito repellents and all beach toys.

Jake stepped off the kerb to follow them.

"Look out!"

In the same instant, there was a scream, the blast of a horn and a screech of tyres behind him. Jake spun round to realise that he was directly in the path of a bus.

Click!

The vehicle was so close that Jake could have reached out and touched it. His heart was pounding in his chest, and he dared not breathe. Jake could see every feature on the face of the startled bus driver, whose eyes were wide open in horror at the thought of the inevitable accident. He was half raised out of his seat as he stood on the brakes and pressed hard on the horn. Smoke from beneath the front tyres hung, eerily frozen, in mid air.

Jake calmed himself with an effort, and looked around the High Street. Several people were looking directly at him, including the woman who had screamed, her mouth open in obvious alarm. Another shopper was in the process of dropping her shopping at the sight of Jake about to be run down.

Further ahead, Jake saw his mum and Alice, both half turned towards the source of the sudden noises. At least they weren't looking directly at him, Jake thought with some relief.

He knew what to do. He pulled out the pocket watch, pushed down on the crown and moved half the minute hand round to the number two. As soon as he released the crown, the Traveller appeared in a flash.

"You called?" he said.

"Oh, Traveller," said Jake. "Boy, am I glad to see you."

"Don't move." Jake stood stock still, just like all the other human statues in the High Street.

The Traveller looked around him and took in the situation rapidly.

"Hmm. That's a bit of a pickle you've got yourself into, Freezer."

"You're telling me," said Jake. "I wasn't concentrating. I was walking along and just stepped into the road without looking. I heard this scream and a loud horn. I saw the bus, and only just had time to react."

"Lucky you've got quick reflexes, I reckon. Another second, I'd say, and you'd have been history."

"Yeah," agreed Jake miserably. "But what can I do now?"

"Well, let's have a look."

The Traveller walked around, taking mental measurements. He walked up and down the road, looking at Jake and the bus from every conceivable angle. Then he came back, shaking his head, to where Jake stood.

"Nothing else for it," he concluded. "You can't move without being seen, but it's a risk we're just going to have to take."

Jake let out a big sigh of relief. Half of him had wondered whether the Traveller would feel obliged to leave him to his fate – and certain death – in order to protect the secret. The Traveller must have read his expression.

"You didn't think we'd let you get run over, did you?" he said.

"Well, I – I thought that protecting the secret was paramount," said Jake.

"Yeah, but it's not something to die for – well, not on this occasion anyway. Otherwise we'd get through Timekeepers like there's no tomorrow, so to speak."

"Phew! That's a relief! But what do we do?"

"Okay, the best thing to do is just to take one step backwards." Jake complied eagerly. "No, that's too much. Forward a bit. Hold it there." The Traveller walked around Jake again, taking more mental measurements.

"Okay, that should do it," he decided.

"Are you sure?" asked Jake. "It still looks awfully close from where I'm standing."

"Sorry, pal, but it's got to. We can't have you suddenly being fifteen feet away, can we? No, I reckon this'll work. Just don't breathe out."

"I'm finding it slightly difficult to breathe at all, actually," said Jake.

"Don't worry. Now, get into the position you were in – you were facing in that direction, but looking at the bus, right?"

Jake tried it, as the Traveller walked round him again, squeezing between Jake and the front of the bus.

"That'll do. Now, keep your hands by your side when you click. I'll disappear when you do, and we'll see what happens. I'll drop by and see you later, and we can see just how much attention you attracted. Ready?"

"As I'll ever be, I s'pose."

"Right, good luck, then," said the Traveller as he stepped back a few paces.

Jake took a deep breath.

Click!

There was a *whoosh!* as the bus screeched past him, inches in front of his eyes. The horn was deafening, and Jake was enveloped in the smoke rising from the front tyres. Luckily for Jake, the bus driver had not attempted to swerve to avoid his original position: the Traveller must have considered that, if the driver was going to swerve, it would more likely be away from Jake's new position.

When the bus came to rest, Jake was standing by its rear tyres and, instinctively now, he jumped backwards onto the kerb.

There seemed to be a second of silence. One woman had fainted, others stood staring at Jake with open-mouthed disbelief, evidently trying to figure out how he had avoided being struck by the bus.

The bus driver opened the door at the front of the bus and came tumbling out, still in shock. He stood gawping at Jake.

"You – I – how…?"

"Jake!"

His mother and Alice appeared behind the driver. They had looked round just in time to see the bus screeching past Jake, but had not known whether he had been hurt.

The bus driver found his voice.

"You were right there in front of me," he said. "I was going to hit you for sure. Then you just seemed to….disappear. I – " He broke off, obviously playing the scene over and over in his mind but unable to comprehend how Jake had managed to escape.

Jake went over to him.

"Sorry," he said. "My own stupid fault. I wasn't looking where I was going."

"But – you just disappeared from view," the driver maintained.

"That's what I thought, too," said a new voice behind him. A crowd was gathering, and Jake started wondering how on earth he could escape this situation. It would have been quite humiliating enough if he had really *just* been missed by the bus, but now people were remembering what they saw. "One second you were standing in the road, right in front of the bus, and the next second you were standing back there. I didn't even see you move."

"Are you alright, Jake?" asked his mother.

"I'm fine, Mum," he said. "Just a lucky escape, I guess. I didn't know my reflexes were that quick, but they must have been."

He turned back to the bus driver.

"Hey, I'm really sorry about that. Are you okay?"

"Yes, I think so. But I still don't understand how – "

Jake decided to take charge of the situation before it deteriorated further.

"C'mon, Mum, let's go."

Several people started talking, but Jake walked politely through the small crowd, pulling his mother's arm and refusing to look anybody in the eye, in case he gave something away. When they were clear, he looked back to see the bus driver still talking animatedly to some of the shoppers. They all seemed to be pointing in different directions at the same time, all of them with confused looks on their faces.

Later that evening, the Traveller dropped in on Jake as he sat watching a video with the rest of his family. It was as if somebody had pressed the 'pause' button not only on the video, but on his parents and sister as well.

"So how did it go?" asked the Traveller.

"Well, I'm still here – just," said Jake. "It was really scary when the bus went past me, but I know it could have been a whole lot worse."

"What about the onlookers?"

"Yeah, there were several of them. The bus driver was the hardest. Stands to reason, I suppose. I mean, I just disappeared right in front of him when we both knew that he should have run me over. He was quite shocked, but he couldn't explain it. A few others started asking questions, but I just apologised for nearly causing an accident and then walked off. It was lucky that my mum and Alice didn't turn round in time to see what happened. It would have been far more difficult to deal with their questions."

The Traveller nodded. "Well, you live and learn. Let's hope you don't find yourself in a similar situation any time soon. You can see how complex things could become if people do see you move – or, rather, *don't* see you move."

"Don't worry," said Jake, "I'll be extra careful in future. It's taught me a valuable lesson, today. But thanks for your help, Traveller. I'm not sure what I'd have done without you."

"No problem, Jake. That's what I'm here for, to help my fellow Timekeepers. Call me if you need to, any time."

And with that, he was gone. The video restarted as if nothing had happened, and Jake sat back in his chair to enjoy it.

CHAPTER NINE

Majorca was baking.

The Heptons had been to the island several times in the past, but rarely ventured into the noisy, touristy enclaves. They preferred to stay in small guesthouses on different parts of the island, savouring the Balearic hospitality and culture.

They had found the beach on the third day of their holiday. It was perfect. Inaccessible by road, the beach was located in a little cove a few hundred metres along the coast from the little village in which they were staying. They had hired a rowing boat, and Jake and his dad had taken it in turns to row to the cove.

There was one other family on the beach – Dutch, Jake thought – but the cove was easily big enough for both of them. The others had arrived in a smart looking motor boat, which was moored offshore, bobbing gently up and down on the tide. Jake's dad studied the boat enviously as they rowed slowly past.

The Heptons lost no time in swimming and playing Frisbee. Alice buried her dad in the sand while Jake explored the rocks surrounding the cove. Having eaten their picnic lunch, they covered themselves in (special offer) high factor sun cream and settled onto their beach towels for a siesta. Relaxation in such a setting was almost guaranteed.

Jake lay there with his eyes closed, enjoying the warmth of the sun on his back and listening to the rhythmic and therapeutic sound of the breaking waves. He guessed that, on average, a wave broke on the beach every five seconds. In between the waves, the silence was unbroken.

It was the silence that eventually disturbed Jake from his slumber. The waves seemed to have stopped. Was he dreaming? He was trying to decide, when a shadow which fell across his face, blocking out the sun. He looked up and squinted at the silhouette.

"Hi, Jake."

"Traveller?" said Jake sleepily.

"Nice place you've found here – lovely beach."

"What're you doing here?" said Jake, sitting up slowly. "Is there a problem?"

"Not sure yet," said Traveller. "But I thought you'd better see this." He produced a thin newspaper from behind his back.

"What is it?"

"It's your local paper, I believe."
"You came all this way to show me my local newspaper?"
"Read it."
Jake looked at the front page and caught his breath.

BOY CHEATS DEATH IN HIGH STREET, BUT HOW?
By Fergus Dingley

"Oh, no," said Jake.
"My reaction entirely," said Traveller. "Read the whole article."

Jake Hepton, a local schoolboy, last week cheated almost certain death in the High Street when he stepped in front of a bus. According to eye witnesses, the teenager had no chance to move out of the path of the oncoming vehicle, but strangely survived completely unscathed.

Bus driver Antonio Gibrello, 52, said: "He was there, right in front of me. I hit the brakes as hard as I could, but I knew it was too late. He suddenly disappeared from view, and I thought I'd hit him, but when I got out I saw him standing by the kerb at the back of the bus. I don't know how he managed it. It was a miracle."

Local resident Ethel Morbey agreed. "I saw him step off the kerb without looking, and I shouted to him. He didn't have a chance. He should have been dead, without a doubt. I didn't see him move, but then there he was, standing beside the back of the bus as if nothing had happened. It was obviously a huge relief that he was unhurt, but I don't know how he did it."

So how did he do it? The teenager was unavailable for comment last night, having apparently gone on holiday with his family. Perhaps it was just a lucky escape, but this reporter discovered from another local resident that Jake Hepton had recently been involved in another strange incident on the High Street, when a petty thief was caught after allegedly running into a lamp post.

Mrs Joan Phippet, 78, had had her handbag snatched in broad daylight, and shouted for help as the thief ran off. "All of a sudden, he dropped the bag and I saw him run straight into the lamp post," she said. "It was really strange. Then this nice boy returned my bag. I'm sure it's the same boy, yes."

Is there a connection between these two incidents? There have been a number of unexplained incidents in this area over the years, all scrupulously recorded by this reporter who believes that it may be the work of the so-called Timekeepers, a shadowy group of individuals with inexplicable power. Some residents continue to scoff at the suggestion that such a group exists, but the evidence is growing. Is this latest incident another piece of the jigsaw?

Jake groaned, and passed the newspaper back to the Traveller.

"This is bad," he said bluntly.

"Bad, yes, but not a total disaster," said Traveller. "Fortunately, most people think that Fergus is a complete nutter. Since he can't explain the concept of the Timekeepers, it's most unlikely that any of his claims will be taken seriously. But then again, it just means that we've got to be really careful. We don't want to give him any more ammunition, do we?"

"No, but how did Fergus find out my name anyway?"

"Well, it's a small town and he's a journalist. It wouldn't have been too difficult for him. He probably spoke to a number of shopkeepers in the High Street: some of them may have been witnesses to the incidents, and it's quite likely that they'd have recognised you and gave him your name."

"So what happens next?" asked Jake.

"Nothing. We just wait for it to blow over, like we have in the past. Besides," said the Traveller, "I asked Seeker to have a look at next week's edition to see if there was any further comment."

"And was there?"

"Yes, but not from Fergus. Several people wrote letters to complain that the front page had been used for such a ridiculous article. One of them said that Fergus should simply be relieved that a dreadful accident had been avoided, rather than suggest nonsense theories about people who can control time. It seems each time he mentions the Timekeepers, fewer people take him seriously. So that's good news for us."

"What about the Master? What did he say about it?"

The Traveller shrugged. "Same as me, really. We Timekeepers can't avoid unfortunate situations – after all, unlike him we're only mortal – and occasionally we have to take risks to protect each other. He's glad you're okay, and asked me to let you know that he's impressed with you so far. You've been far more restrained than most other new Timekeepers: I quite often need to visit them to remind them of the rules."

"Well, that's nice to know, I suppose."

"Exactly. Don't worry about it." The Traveller looked up at the blazing sun. "Well, I'd best be off. I think I'm a bit overdressed for the beach anyway." He stood up and brushed sand off the seat of his trousers. "Enjoy the rest of your holiday, won't you?"

"I don't think that'll be too hard," said Jake as he lay back down on his towel.

"Lucky blighter," muttered the Traveller. "See you later, then."

The Traveller vanished, and the next wave broke on the beach.

The holiday – like any holiday – passed too quickly, and the Heptons soon arrived back at home happy, relaxed and refreshed. The taxi turned into Duckworth Close, and it suddenly seemed as though they had hardly been away.

The post had mounted up on the doormat over the last week. A fair amount of junk mail was thrown away immediately. Jake found a couple of letters addressed to him. He opened the first to find a card from Uncle Thomas and Auntie Maureen, congratulating him on his exam success and enclosing a cheque for fifty pounds. Cool, thought Jake, already spending the money in his mind on CDs and computer games.

His short reverie was interrupted by his mother.

"Jake!" she called. "Come and look at this!"

Jake went into the kitchen to find his parents and Alice standing around the kitchen table.

"You're on the front page of the local newspaper," said his mother.

"Yeah, I know," said Jake.

"What do you mean, you know?" asked his father. "I've only just opened it. Look – *"Boy cheats death in High Street, but how?"* Front page."

Whoops, thought Jake. That was dumb of me.

"I mean – um – I'm not surprised. Not much happens round here, so I'm not surprised that an incident like that in the High Street is headline news."

His father went on. "It also says that you were involved when that old lady's bag was snatched, and claims that it's got something to do with the Timekeepers – *"A shadowy group of individuals with inexplicable powers"*. Huh! Preposterous bloody idea!"

"The Timekeepers," said his mother. "Fergus Dingley – of course. You must remember, dear. Fergus Dingley is that journalist who first wrote about the Timekeepers. He had a big run-in with Mr Walker about it, though why he thought a nice old man like Mr Walker might have secret powers over time is quite beyond me."

"You're right," said Jake's father. "God, what was the editor thinking of, giving space on the front page to a cretin like Fergus Dingley? He got crucified by his media colleagues when he first made those bizarre claims, didn't he? I'm surprised he ever found another job." He walked out of the kitchen towards the living room, reading the paper as he went.

"Right," said Jake's mother. "A nice cup of tea before we start unpacking, I think.." And she put the kettle on.

Jake told his mother about the cheque from Uncle Thomas.

"That's kind of them," she said. "You'll have to write and say thank you. Who's that other letter from?"

Jake looked at the other letter he had put on the kitchen table. "I don't know. I haven't opened it yet." He took his tea and walked through to the living room. He sat down on the sofa and opened the other envelope.

The letter was typed.

Dear Mr Hepton,

As a freelance journalist, I wrote the article in this week's Gazette about the incident in the High Street in which you were involved recently. I understand you are on holiday as I write, but I hope that we might have the opportunity to meet soon after your return.

I am particularly interested to learn your account of the incident. Having spoken to several eye witnesses, I can only conclude that something very strange took place for which some degree of further explanation is required. Your help in this regard would be invaluable.

I would be most grateful if you could contact me on the above telephone number to confirm receipt of this letter, and to arrange a mutually convenient time for a meeting. I would of course be happy to reimburse you for your time, and I look forward to hearing from you shortly.

Your sincerely

Fergus Dingley

Jake stared at the letter. Oh no, he thought, Fergus Dingley wants a meeting! He tried to think rationally about what to do. On the one hand, it could be a perfectly innocent request. Fergus was hardly accusing him of being a Timekeeper, and was probably just following up a story. It might be rude if Jake didn't acknowledge the letter, or if he declined a meeting. On the other hand, declining a meeting might make Fergus think that Jake had something to hide. And if such a meeting did take place, would Jake be able to act convincingly enough to fool Fergus? He was, after all, an experienced journalist. Jake couldn't afford to make a mistake.

He needed some advice, but he decided that he'd go and discuss it with Mr Walker first, rather than call on the Traveller. Mr Walker had personal experience of dealing with Fergus, so his advice would be reliable.

Jake decided not to mention the letter to his parents yet, at least not until he had spoken to Mr Walker. His father would probably call Fergus himself, telling him to leave his son alone. No, he couldn't involve his parents yet.

It was still only the middle of the afternoon, and the unpacking had all been done. Jake's mother had a mountain of washing and ironing to do, whilst his father had been sent out to the supermarket to stock up.

"I think I'll go over and see Mr Walker," said Jake. "He asked me to tell him about our holiday when we got back."

"Fine," said his mother without looking up from the ironing board. "We'll have supper about seven, so don't be late."

Jake trotted over the road. He had lots to talk about, and Mr Walker had no doubt seen a copy of the local paper himself. That was confirmed when the door opened and Mr Walker said, "Ah, if it isn't the local hero with mysterious power to cheat death – and quite a tanned local hero, too!"

Jake smiled. "Traveller came to see me in Majorca to tell me about it," he said. "It's not exactly the type of publicity to be proud of." Mr Walker closed the door, and Jake followed him into the living room.

"So what did Traveller say about it?"

"Well, he was there at the time. I called him when it looked like I was about to be hit by that bus."

"Good move. It never does any harm to call for help."

"He helped me out, but we knew it couldn't be done without something being noticed. I didn't think that Fergus Dingley would have got hold of the story, though. Traveller asked Seeker to have a look at this week's edition and, fortunately, nobody's taking him seriously. Even my dad said that Fergus is a lunatic."

Mr Walker sighed. "Ah, well, I suppose it's for the best. It's such a shame, though, since we both know that Fergus is right. He was a friend

59

of mine for many years – although he doesn't know it – and it pains me to see him being discredited like this."

"What do you think I should do?" asked Jake. "Should I meet him?"

"Hmm, that's a tough one. If you weren't a Timekeeper, you'd probably agree with your father, and say no. But since you *are* a Timekeeper, I'm not sure you have much choice. It could be a difficult meeting, but at least it would allow you to get an idea of what Fergus is thinking and, if he intends to make a real nuisance of himself again, that sort of intelligence could be useful for you and your colleagues."

"I guess you're right," sighed Jake. "I'll call the Traveller and let him know. If he agrees, I'll meet Fergus. I don't know what my parents will say, though."

"Look at it this way," said Mr Walker. "It's not every day that a journalist asks you for an interview, so it could be an interesting experience. And Fergus says he's willing to reimburse you for your time – how bad can that be? It won't be a huge sum, but I don't know many teenagers that would turn down the opportunity to make some easy money like that, and get some interesting experience at the same time."

Jake smiled. "You're right. I could always use some extra cash. Besides, if the questions get too difficult, I can always ask the Traveller for some advice on how to answer."

"Indeed. But you'd obviously have to be very careful about it. It would be quite risky to freeze time when you're sitting opposite a journalist – especially one like Fergus Dingley who will be watching every move you make to see if he can add weight to his theories."

"Yeah, that could be tricky. But if I can throw Fergus off the scent, perhaps he won't be too inquisitive about me in the future."

"Mmm, don't bet on it. Once Fergus is on a trail, it's hard to distract him. Having been discredited already, he doesn't have much to lose anyway." His expression brightened. "So, come on, tell me about your holiday."

CHAPTER TEN

When Jake got home, he went up to his bedroom and contacted the Traveller. He didn't need the privacy of his room, but somehow he felt more secure.

The Traveller appeared at once, and Jake told him about the letter from Fergus Dingley and his conversation with Mr Walker. The Traveller read the letter and nodded.

"I agree you should meet him," he said. "I think it would also be worth calling a meeting with the others, just so they know the situation. They all know Fergus, of course, and it may be that they'll need to be involved at a later stage. I doubt he'll give up trying to expose the Timekeepers. I don't think he's got malicious intentions, but he obviously knows something is going on which he can't explain, and he's probably getting more frustrated that nobody is taking him seriously. Let's say we'll meet in ten minutes? I'll contact the others to let them know."

"Sure," said Jake. The Traveller disappeared.

Ten minutes, thought Jake, looking at his pocket watch. That just about gives me enough time for a triple decker sandwich.

At the appointed time, Jake returned to his room and picked up the letter from Fergus. He pressed down on the crown of the pocket watch, and carefully moved half of the minute hand round to the number six. He released the pressure, and instantly found himself standing in the strange windowless room.

He was alone, but there was a serene atmosphere in the brightly lit room, and Jake didn't feel anxious. Within seconds, the other five Timekeepers appeared simultaneously, forming a natural circle.

"Timekeepers, welcome," said the Master. He pushed back his great hood and looked at Jake.

"Freezer, you have gathered us together. The Traveller has informed me of the purpose, but I would ask you to explain the circumstances in which we meet."

"Thank you, Master," said Jake. He looked around the room, and saw that all eyes were on him. "The Traveller and I thought it would be useful to call a meeting to discuss Fergus Dingley, who wrote an article the other week mentioning the Timekeepers. I'm afraid it was my fault that he wrote that article – I almost got run over by a bus, and it was impossible to get out of the way without somebody noticing. I'm sorry for that," he said, looking at the Master.

"We're not here to judge, Freezer. It was an unfortunate incident, but all your colleagues have found themselves in similar predicaments over the years." All the others nodded. "So no blame is attached. These things happen, and we deal with them. Please, go on."

"Well, when I got back from holiday, there was this letter from Fergus." He passed the letter to the Traveller on his left, who passed it on to the Master. The Master glanced at it as Jake continued. "He wants to meet me. I discussed it with Mr Walker, who probably knows Fergus better than any of us, and he thinks that I should agree to a meeting. If I don't meet him, Fergus might assume that I know something which I don't want to tell him, so it might be easier to pretend that I don't know what he's talking about. I'd like to know what others think, since you've all had experience in dealing with Fergus in the past."

"Thank you, Freezer," said the Master. He looked around the circle. "Any views?"

"I agree with Mr Walker," said Retro. "Fergus isn't going to give up making these claims, is he? Few people believe him, but he still keeps writing these articles. He knows something is going on, but he can't explain it. So I think our best bet would be to hear what he has to say, and try to handle it accordingly." She looked across at Jake. "By the way, Freezer, don't feel bad about the bus – I broke several bones in a car accident last year, and Traveller took me back and made sure I *didn't* take my eyes off the road!"

Seeker was next. "I think Mr Walker's advice was spot on, too. Let's all stay in touch during the meeting, and I can keep an eye on what Fergus is going to write afterwards. That way, we can try to limit any further damage."

"Good point, Seeker" said the Traveller. "Splitter?"

"Yeah, I'm up for it as well. Let's do it."

"We are agreed, then," concluded the Master. "Freezer, please arrange to meet Fergus at your convenience. The Traveller will be standing by, and can relay any messages to the rest of us. We'll help you through it, if necessary." He passed the letter back round to Jake, who folded it and put it in his pocket.

"Thank you, Master," said Jake. "I'll try not to let you down."

"I have no concerns about that, Freezer. Let us all adjourn, then. We shall meet again before too long." He vanished, signalling an end to the formal meeting.

"Are you okay, Jake?" asked the Seeker.

"Yes, I think so."

"It'll be quite a test for you, meeting Fergus. We all know him already, of course, but you haven't had that pleasure yet. Don't worry about it – you'll be fine."

"Okay," said the Traveller. "Let's get going. Jake, I'll be waiting for your call."

All five took out their pocket watches, pressed down on the crown and reunited the two halves of the minute hands. One by one, they all disappeared.

In an instant, Jake was back in his room. He went downstairs and told his parents about the letter from Fergus.

"Bloody man!" said his father. "What would you want to meet him for?"

"Well, I know it's hardly a big story – "

"No, it's hardly a story at all. People controlling time? Nonsense!"

"I'd like to meet him all the same," insisted Jake.

"Why?"

"Well, he asked to hear my side of the story, and he's going to pay me for it. My side of the story is that I had quick reflexes, and just managed to jump clear in time. If a journalist's going to pay me to hear that, it sounds like a good deal to me."

"Fair point," his father conceded. "If the man is willing to pay for that, he's even more bonkers than I thought."

"And it would be good experience anyway, being interviewed by a journalist. It might be a career option for me to consider."

His father almost choked on his tea. "God, I hope not. Serious journalism has its place, but so many journalists nowadays are just working for the gutter press, nosing around in the private affairs of ordinary people and coming up with stories that hardly deserve printing. I mean, just look at the rubbish in this," he said, waving the local paper.

"Well, it's a small town," said Jake. "It's hardly the same as working for a national paper, is it?"

"So, are you happy to meet this Dingley bloke on your own, or do you want me to come along too?"

"Would you keep quiet, if you were there?"

"Probably not – not if he starts asking stupid questions and making ridiculous allegations about individuals with secret powers."

"Then I'd rather do it alone, thanks," said Jake.

His father muttered something inaudible about 'bloody waste of time', and switched on the television to watch the news. Jake got up and went into the hallway. He picked up the phone, and dialled the number at the top of the letter.

It was answered almost immediately.

"Dingley!"

The voice sounded gruff and impatient, almost as if the incoming call was a nuisance.

"Er – hi, it's Jake Hepton here."

"Jake Hepton? Jake Hepton….Oh, yes, Jake Hepton." The gruffness and impatience disappeared as Fergus put on a warmer voice. "Thank you so much for calling. How was your holiday?"

"Fine, thank you," said Jake politely. He didn't want to get into a conversation about his holiday, so he went straight to the point. "You said you'd like to meet me to talk about that incident in the High Street."

"Indeed, yes," said Fergus. "I'd very much like to hear your version of events. Several things just don't seem to add up."

"Well, I'm not sure if I can help you much. It was very lucky that I managed to jump out of the way in time, and that's just about all there is to it."

"Hmm." There was a short pause. "All the same, I think we should meet. Just so that I can get the complete picture. Would tomorrow be convenient for you?"

"Okay," said Jake. "What sort of time?"

"Time, yes." There was another short pause, almost as if every mention of the word 'time' made Fergus stop and think. "How about eleven o'clock? We could meet in that new café in the High Street – what's it called? – The Coffee Pot."

"Yeah, I know it. I'll see you there at eleven tomorrow then."

"Excellent, excellent. I look forward to meeting you."

"Bye." Jake hung up, and returned to his room. It was strange: for the first time since he could remember, he felt as if he was facing a test for which he was entirely unprepared. He lay on his bed and thought about what lay ahead.

After a sleepless night, Jake felt no better. He knew that the Traveller would be there to help if necessary, but that was small consolation. He couldn't afford to say anything which might encourage Fergus to think that his suspicions were correct. If he did, it would be very hard to put right.

He arrived at the café ten minutes early, and ordered a cup of tea. There were only three other people there: two old ladies sharing a huge iced bun, both trying desperately to eat it as delicately as possible with the inadequate plastic forks provided; and a young mother who sat there looking blank and exhausted while her baby slept contentedly in its pushchair. Jake sat at one of the tables at the back, facing the street. From there, he could see any new customer who walked in. A middle aged couple stopped to read the menu displayed in the window before moving on.

After a few minutes, a man walked in. He looked sweaty and slightly out of breath, as if he had been hurrying. His tie was done up loosely, the top button of his shirt was undone, and his cuffs were rolled back. His dark curly hair was greying and receding, and he had a ruddy complexion, probably due to the haste in which he had arrived. His weary appearance was one of a busy and overworked executive. He carried a black bag on a shoulder strap – a laptop computer, Jake decided.

The man looked at Jake sitting on his own, and came straight over.

"Jake?" he asked.

"Yes. You must be Mr Dingley."

"Fergus, please," he said, as he put down his shoulder bag and shook Jake's hand. "Good to meet you. Now, let me get a coffee – can I get anything for you?"

"No, I'm fine thanks," said Jake.

Fergus wiped his brow and set off for the counter. He fumbled in his pockets for change and handed it over before returning to the table with a steaming cup of black coffee. He sat down and added three small packets of sugar.

"Well, now, Jake," he said in a pleasant tone as he mindlessly stirred his coffee. "It's nice to put a face to the name. You caused quite some excitement the other week, eh? Everyone was talking about it – your lucky escape."

"Were they?" asked Jake, trying to sound casual but not too dismissive. "It didn't seem a big thing at the time. As you said, it was just a lucky escape. I was amazed that you wrote about it, actually."

"It was a newsworthy item."

"Really?" said Jake.

Fergus had obviously practiced his lines. "Well, of course, if the bus had just missed you, it would hardly have deserved a mention. What made it interesting – and, from my point of view, newsworthy – was that the bus *shouldn't* have missed you at all."

"How do you mean?" asked Jake.

"By all accounts – and I had several to choose from – you shouldn't have been able to get out of the way. You were seen, in the blink of an eye, to move from one spot to another without jumping, or indeed without making any discernible movement at all. What I want to know is, how did you manage that? Personally, I think that the Timekeepers had something to do with it."

"Timekeepers?" asked Jake. His heart was thumping, and he was sure he was blushing as he feigned ignorance of the Timekeepers.

"Have you heard of them?"

"Um…I think I read something about them a while ago – ," said Jake.

"Must've been one of my articles. Not many people agree with me, but I know such a group exists. I don't know how I know, and I don't yet have any proof, but I know!"

"So who belongs to this group?"

"Again, I don't know – yet," said Fergus, realising that his idea was, once again, beginning to sound foolish.

Jake raised his eyebrows. "I must say, it all sounds rather weird. You say that a group of Timekeepers exists, but you don't have any proof, and you don't know who's in it. You don't even know how you know – "

Fergus had heard variations of such scepticism regularly and, as always, had to keep hold of his patience.

"I know it sounds ridiculous – crazy, insane, whatever you want to call it – but, please, let me tell you what I *do* know." There was almost a pleading in his eyes. Poor guy, thought Jake. He doesn't even know how right he is, and yet people think he's nuts. He can't get anybody to believe him. After a moment, Jake sat back and folded his arms. He nodded.

"Thank you," breathed Fergus. He paused. He'd been in this situation so often before: he had found somebody willing to listen, but they always ended up concluding that it was all a fantasy. All he wanted was for somebody, somewhere, sometime, to say, "Yes, something strange *is* happening". He looked at Jake, trying to ascertain whether he could see genuine interest in his eyes, or bored acceptance that he was about to be lectured on something that would simply be a waste of time. He couldn't decide, but he was sure the boy was somehow different to others who had offered him the chance to air his views.

"Have you lived around here all your life?" he asked.

"Yes," said Jake simply.

"Then I hope you'll agree that, over the years, there have been a number of – what shall we call them – 'strange happenings' in this town."

"Like what?" asked Jake. He'd never thought about it before, and now tried to think of previous events in which Mr Walker or his other colleagues might have played a role.

"Let me show you. I've been compiling a list of these bizarre occurrences," said Fergus, taking the laptop computer from its case. He laid it on the table between them, opened it and switched it on. Neither spoke while the computer warmed up.

Fergus tapped a few keys, and swivelled the computer around so that Jake could see the screen too.

"Here. I've catalogued a number of weird events which have happened around here over the last twenty years. I've got another collection, at home, of press cuttings from around the world which describe similarly inexplicable happenings."

Jake quickly scanned the document on the screen in front of him. It was neatly compiled, giving a serial number, a date, time and place, and details of the unusual event. There were also witness testimonies beside some of the entries. One which caught Jake's eye read: "My pushchair fell into the canal with the baby in it. I didn't know what to do. I can't swim, so I just started screaming. A few seconds later, I heard my baby crying behind me. I looked round and saw the pushchair just a few feet away, dripping wet. The baby was still strapped in, but completely unharmed. I couldn't believe it. I don't know how it happened, but I was just so relieved to get my baby back safe and sound. It was a miracle."

"So you reckon this list of events is evidence that some strange group – the Timekeepers – really exists?" asked Jake.

"That's right," said Fergus, wondering whether he might at last have convinced someone of his theory. "The list isn't exhaustive, by any means. There must be hundreds of similar events which have gone undocumented. These are just the ones I've come across. This list might represent just the tip of the iceberg." He paused, as if allowing time for the statement to sink in. "These cases *are* all connected, somehow. There are one or two on the same day, in the same area, then nothing for months. It's more than coincidence, I'm sure of it."

"Well, Mr Dingley – "

"Fergus, please."

"Fergus." Jake paused briefly. "It's interesting, but I don't see how I can be of any help to you – "

"Ah, but I think you can," said Fergus.

"How?"

Fergus's stare made Jake feel quite uncomfortable. He tried not to show any unease, but wondered where Fergus was heading.

"You've been an enormous help already, Jake. You see, you're different."

"Different? What do you mean?" asked Jake. He was sure he saw a glint in Fergus' eyes.

"I said that all these events were connected, that coincidence could almost certainly be ruled out."

"So?" said Jake.

"Well, there are similarities between them all," Fergus continued. "In each case, there's at least one main subject and a number of witnesses. The statements of the witnesses are all similar, in that they all attest to having seen something totally inexplicable take place – like people or objects disappearing from one place and reappearing in another in an instant. The statements of the individual main subjects are also similar. Like the witnesses, they are at a loss to explain what happened. They acknowledge that something did happen, but they are just as perplexed as those who witnessed the event."

"Why does that make me different?" asked Jake, at the same instant as he realised where Fergus was heading.

"There were a number of witnesses to the incidents in the High Street in which you were involved. Let's forget the petty thief for the moment, and concentrate on what you insist was just a "lucky escape" from certain death. A number of people saw, from a variety of angles, what happened. They know what they saw, and I'm inclined to believe them. What puzzles me, therefore, is your own reaction."

Jake hoped desperately that his expression gave nothing away, as Fergus continued.

"You still maintain that you were just fortunate, that you had quick reflexes, and that you managed to jump out of the way just in time. Why would you do that?"

Jake swallowed. "Because it's the truth, of course."

"Is it?" asked Fergus. "Not a single witness agrees with you. Not one of them saw you move. How likely is that? Nobody's reflexes are *that* quick. No, I'm afraid I don't believe it. But then, why would you lie? Either you know exactly what did happen or – "

"Or what?" asked Jake, not sure that he wanted to hear the response.

"My goodness," whispered Fergus. "Is it possible?"

"What?" insisted Jake.

"Is it possible that – you – you are a Timekeeper?"

CHAPTER ELEVEN

Click!

Fergus, and everything else, froze.

My God, thought Jake, breathing hard. He had expected Fergus to challenge his version of what had happened, but he hadn't prepared himself for this. If Fergus suspected Jake of being a Timekeeper, that could be disastrous. He needed to discuss it with the Traveller. He took out the pocket watch, turned half of the minute hand round to the number two, and released the crown.

"Hey, Jake," said a familiar voice. "I was waiting for you to call."

"Hi, Traveller," said Jake. The Traveller sat on the edge of the table next to Jake's, being careful not to move the chairs out of position.

"So you've met Fergus – I must say, he's looking a little less healthy than last time I saw him. He's put on a fair amount of weight. Still, how's it going?" he asked, looking back at Jake.

"Not good, I'm afraid." Jake took the Traveller through his conversation with Fergus so far, and the Traveller leaned forward to study the document displayed on Fergus' computer.

"He's certainly done his homework, hasn't he?" he said. "Fortunately, he's missing quite a few from his list, but let's not enlighten him, eh?"

Jake smiled. The humour broke the tension for him slightly.

"So what should I do?" he asked.

"Simple, really. You've got to stick to your story. Tell him he's crazy if he thinks that you're really a Timekeeper – he'll probably expect to be told that anyway. If the worst came to the worst, I suppose Retro and I could take him back in time so that you could start the conversation again. We could delete the document on his computer, but that might arouse his suspicions further if we did that now, and he's probably got a spare copy somewhere. I think your best bet is to hold your line. That probably stands more chance of getting Fergus to question himself yet again about whether he really is making it all up. It won't throw him off for long, I shouldn't think, but it'll do for the moment."

"Yeah, I guess you're right," agreed Jake. "I don't fancy extending this conversation for longer than necessary anyway, so maybe I'll just finish it and walk out."

"Okay, but don't be angry about it – that'd make him think you're hiding something. Do it calmly."

"Alright," said Jake. "Thanks for the advice. I'll let you know how it goes, and I'd like to talk it over with Mr Walker too, if that's okay with you."

"Sure it is," said the Traveller. "Right, back into position, and I'll be off."

"See you soon – and thanks again."

"Bye, Jake."

Click!

Jake raised his eyebrows. "Me? A Timekeeper? I wish!"

"Well, it all fits," said Fergus, apparently getting quite excited as he tried to justify his accusation. "Your reaction is quite different to others on this list. You'd only do that if you knew more than you're letting on. If you knew something about the Timekeepers, you'd tell me – unless you're one of them!"

Jake stood up suddenly, but maintained a calm voice.

"Mr Dingley, I – "

"Fergus, please!"

"*Mister Dingley*, I don't want to be rude, but that's a crazy idea. I agreed to meet you to let you have my version of events when I was nearly run over, and I've done that. Now you're suggesting that I'm a Timekeeper – I'm sorry, but I really don't think we've got anything else to discuss."

"Now just hold on a min – "

"No, I'm sorry, but I've given you what you asked for, and I'd like to leave now. By the way, you said you'd pay me?"

Fergus' eyes narrowed for a second, before he pulled his wallet from his jacket pocket and took out a £20 note. He put it on the table between them, but kept his hand on top of it.

"So I'm wrong, am I?" he asked.

"What – yes, you are," said Jake firmly.

"We'll see," said Fergus. "I live round here too, you know, and I'll be watching you."

Jake was about to remind Fergus that he'd already had a restraining order put on him for harassing Mr Walker, but he managed to bite his tongue. He wasn't meant to know that, and he certainly didn't want Fergus knowing that Mr Walker was a close friend. That would make matters far worse.

"Is that a threat?" he asked.

"No, no – " began Fergus.

"Good, because I used to be bullied at school, and it's not fun. I put a stop to that, and if I see you following me around, I'll call the police, right? I've done what you asked of me today, and I haven't got any more to say to you, I'm afraid."

He took a corner of the note under Fergus' hand and pulled it out. He stared at Fergus for a second before turning and walking to the door, hoping desperately that he looked more confident than he felt. He glanced back as he opened the door. Fergus was looking after him with a puzzled look on his red face. Jake strode out and, once out of sight of the café, ran off through the park to see Mr Walker.

"Jake – goodness, you look all out of breath. Has something happened?"

"Fergus Dingley," said Jake.

"Ah. Well, you'd better come in and tell me about it."

When he had finished, Mr Walker sighed.

"Oh dear," he said. "It sounds as if Fergus might start making a nuisance of himself again. Still, I think you did the right thing, meeting him. I'm afraid it'll only be a matter of time before he connects you to me – indeed, he's probably done that already, since he knows both of our addresses."

"Of course," said Jake. "That must be why he assumed I might be a Timekeeper."

"We still have one advantage, though."

"What's that?"

"Proof," said Mr Walker. "Fergus doesn't have any, and every time he writes an article on the subject, he seems to make even more enemies."

"But he's not going to give up, is he?" Jake asked, more to confirm his suspicions than in real hope.

"No. That's why you've got to be even more careful from now on. He'll be looking for any scrap of evidence to support his claims – nothing would make him happier. But if he does start following you around, you should carry out your threat and call the police. Get it sorted quickly. Apart from anything else, something like that would damage his reputation further. If he gets any real evidence, it could be most disturbing."

"I'll try not to give him the chance," said Jake.

"A word of advice, Jake. Do keep your colleagues closely informed. They'll need to be aware of what's happening."

"Don't worry, I will. I think I'm going to need all the help I can get."

On the short walk home, Jake kept looking anxiously around. He was sure he'd seen a movement out of the corner of his eye when he left Mr Walker's house. He wondered if he was just being paranoid, and decided there was no harm in checking.

Click!

He checked his position carefully, and set off towards the main road. As he passed each driveway, he looked behind hedges and cars, satisfying himself that nobody was there. Just before the junction with the main road, an empty car was parked on the side of the road. It was a battered old thing which had clearly seen better days, and it contrasted strongly with the new car parked on the driveway. Still, Jake decided, perhaps it belonged to the student son of Mr and Mrs Davies, who lived at number three.

He walked past it and found Fergus, frozen in a crouching position whilst pretending to tie his shoe laces. It wasn't a huge surprise to Jake, even though it confirmed his worst fears. So Fergus was watching him, or perhaps watching Mr Walker. Either way, he would have seen Jake leaving Mr Walker's house.

But, thought Jake, at least he doesn't know that I know. I can stop and check any time I like. He was about to turn back when an idea struck him. It was risky, but he just couldn't resist it.

He went around the hedge of number three, and scooped up a handful of soft soil. Being careful not to drop any, he returned to Fergus' car and, crouching down next to Fergus, put the soil in the exhaust pipe. He went back for a second handful, and packed the pipe until it was solid. He brushed away a few grains of dirt from the ground beneath the exhaust, and checked for any other tell-tale signs. There were none, so Jake trotted back to his original position.

Click!

He carried on walking, without looking back again, and entered his own house. He could see the rest of the family in the back garden, so he went into the front room, which was empty. He stood back from the window, sure that the net curtains would obscure the view of Fergus or anybody else trying to look into the room, especially from a distance and in bright sunlight.

73

After a few moments, he saw Fergus get into the car. The engine turned over, but did not start. Fergus tried it again. He obviously didn't suspect anything was amiss: the car was so old that it would probably have been a surprise if it had started first time. All of a sudden there was a loud *bang* as the car backfired, a cloud of soil and smoke erupting from the rear.

Fergus jumped out of the car and ran round to the back, trying to determine what had happened. Mr Davies emerged from number three and looked disapprovingly at the car. He presumably asked Fergus if everything was alright, and Jake saw Fergus shrug his shoulders. He hurriedly got back in the car, turned the ignition, and it started. Mr Davies shook his head and went back indoors. Fergus turned the car around, and headed off, turning out of Duckworth Close with a squeal of tyres.

Gotcha, thought Jake. But next time it'll be the police. He smiled to himself and went out into the garden to join the rest of his family.

Not long after supper, when the Hepton family were once again gathered in front of the television, the Traveller appeared.

"So how did it go with Fergus after I left?" he asked.

Jake had now got used to the Traveller appearing out of the blue, and he no longer felt uncomfortable talking openly with him while his family sat frozen, in splendid ignorance, around him. He told him how the meeting had ended, and about his subsequent discovery of Fergus watching him. The Traveller listened carefully.

"It's unlikely he'll suspect that you had anything to do with his car backfiring," said the Traveller when Jake had finished, "but all the same, best to tread carefully from now on. If you see him watching you, challenge him. Don't stop time, just give him a final warning that you'll call the police if you see him following you again. After all the trouble he got into for harassing Mr Walker, he won't want to run the risk getting arrested for doing the same to you. If he's sensible, he'll take the threat seriously."

"Okay," said Jake.

"Good. Oh, one other thing. There's been a meeting called for tonight, at eleven o'clock sharp."

"Why so late?" asked Jake.

"Because you should be in bed by then, and nobody will miss you."

"But they wouldn't miss me anyway," said Jake. "Time stops, doesn't it?"

"Normally, yes," explained the Traveller. "But this is an emergency operation, and we'll need to take you somewhere else. You'll need to stop and start time, so we'll have to do that when we'd all normally be asleep, just in case."

Jake was puzzled. "I don't follow you. If it's an emergency, shouldn't we act now?"

"No, it's not an emergency yet, but it will be," said the Traveller. "The meeting's been called by Seeker – she'll explain everything later, you'll see." He looked at his watch – rather pointlessly, Jake thought – and said: "Well, better be off, I've still got to contact the others. Back in position now." Jake had barely moved. "Yeah, that'll do. See you in a little while." And with that, he vanished.

CHAPTER TWELVE

Time seemed to drag. Jake went up to his room at ten o'clock. He wasn't tired, but there was nothing on television and he couldn't concentrate anyway. He'd been wondering what the meeting would be about. He turned on the computer and loaded his favourite game, but it didn't distract him enough. He picked up a book and read the same paragraph three times before giving up and lobbing it back onto the shelf. He put on some rock music, turning the volume down low so that it wouldn't be heard by anybody else in the house, then lay on his bed with his arms behind his head, staring at the ceiling. Every few minutes, he checked his watch.

Eventually, it was time to go. He took out the pocket watch, pushed down the crown and turned half of the minute hand to the number six. When the other half of the minute hand hit the number twelve, he released the crown and vanished.

Seeker and Traveller were already there, and Retro and Splitter turned up fractionally after Jake. When they were all gathered, the Master appeared.

"Timekeepers, thank you for coming together at such a late hour," he said. "Seeker, you have called this meeting – please, inform us of the circumstances."

All eyes turned towards the Seeker.

"Thank you, Master," she began. "I was cruising tonight, and came across a disastrous event in three weeks' time." She held up the front page of a newspaper, which read:

DISASTER AT HEATHROW: PASSENGER JET CRASHES, KILLING 460

There was a gasp around the room. The Seeker continued.

"It says that the front wheel failed to drop down and, having tried all other emergency procedures, the pilots attempted an emergency crash landing. But the plane skidded and lost control, and the sparks from the front of the plane started a catastrophic fire. Everybody on board was killed."

Jake was horrified. He looked around the room, seeing similar expressions on Retro and Splitter. Strangely, though, Traveller and the Master were impassive.

"But I think we might be able to help," said Seeker, "so I discussed it with the Traveller."

The Traveller took over.

"Yes, I reckon we can change things to save the lives of everybody on board," he said, looking around the room. "We're all going to have to work together on this one. We'll need to try something very tricky and we won't know if it'll work until afterwards, when Seeker can check again. We'll go now, and I'll brief you when we get there."

"Good luck," said the Master. "I hope you're successful, and I look forward to a positive report later." He bowed his head and vanished.

"Right," said the Traveller. "The rest of us need to link arms." All five of them stood in a tight circle with arms interlinked.

"Seeker, Splitter, you need to click together." They nodded. "Splitter, take us to the site of the crash. Seeker, make it a few minutes before the crash happens. Freezer, as soon as we arrive, stop time, okay?" Jake nodded. "Ready, on my count – one, two, three – now!"

Instantly, the group was standing on the runway at Heathrow.

Click!

Jake's timing was good. They hardly had time to hear the sound of planes taking off from a nearby runway before there was instant silence. The darkness concealed them effectively. At the end of the runway on which they stood, they saw the blue and orange lights of the emergency vehicles in the middle of the preparations for the impending crash landing.

Jake broke the silence. "What would have happened if it had been daylight?" he asked.

"I discussed that with the Master," said the Traveller. "We wouldn't have been able to do anything. You can't have a group of people suddenly appearing in the middle of the runway in broad daylight."

"You mean – " began Jake.

"Yes, I'm afraid we'd have had to let it happen," said the Traveller. "So, lucky for us, and the plane load of passengers, that it's night time. I still don't know if my plan will work, but we've got to give it a shot, haven't we? Right, let's walk that way a bit. We need to get in the right position."

The group unlinked their arms, and walked down the runway, away from the emergency vehicles. After a couple of minutes, the Traveller brought them to a halt.

"Okay, by my calculations, I reckon this is about the place where the plane should touch down. You can see the landing lights of the plane there, in the distance." Everybody looked up, and saw two bright white lights shining in their direction.

"Jake," said the Traveller, "you'll need to start time again when I give the word, but be ready to stop it again whenever I say. Got that?"

"Sure," said Jake. "But – what's the plan, Traveller?"

"Ah, yes, I should tell you that," said the Traveller. "I'm going to try to pull the front wheel down manually, just before touchdown."

"You what?" said Splitter, incredulously. "Are you mad? Do you know anything about planes?"

"Actually, I do," replied the Traveller. "I'm an aircraft engineer in real life, so I know a thing or two about them."

"Blimey, that's handy," said Retro. "Fancy being able to use your ordinary skills to save lives as a Timekeeper – if you know what I mean."

It dawned on Jake that he didn't know what any of their professions were. The Seeker looked like a school teacher or a librarian, the Splitter looked, well, unemployable, and the Retro looked like a fashion model. He made a mental note to ask them at some point, but now wasn't the right time.

"Yeah, I thought so," said the Traveller, smiling. "Thank goodness it wasn't something involving ships instead – I get terrible sea sickness." The others laughed. "Okay, are you ready, Jake?"

"Ready."

Click!

The noise of jet engines resumed as planes took off. At the end of the runway on which they stood, they could faintly hear the sirens of the emergency vehicles, whose lights had now started flashing again. The two bright white lights on the front of the doomed jet drew slowly closer and lower.

A spotlight on the roof of the control tower was switched on, illuminating the aircraft as it descended.

"Bugger, I hadn't though of that," said the Traveller.

"Is that a problem?" asked the Seeker.

"Not really. It would have been good to stand on the runway so that we can get the exact spot, but we can hardly do that with a spotlight on us. Never mind, we'll just have to stand by the side of the runway, on the dark side away from the control tower. Jake, you'll have to click more often than I thought, I'm afraid, so we can get it right."

"No worries," said Jake. They scampered off the runway, and crouched down in a grass ditch that ran parallel.

They watched as the plane descended lower. It looked massive from this angle, thought Jake. The Traveller's hand rested on Jake's arm.

"When I tap your arm, click," he said. "With the noise of the engines, you won't hear me if I shout the command."

"Good point," said Jake.

They watched silently as the rear wheels of the plane touched down a few hundred metres away from them, its nose still high in the air.

"The pilot will want to keep the nose up for as long as possible," the Traveller explained, "so that he can decrease the speed as much as he can before he has to bring the nose down."

The jet approached them at what seemed like an amazing speed, and Jake saw the nose of the plane begin to descend. There was a tap on his arm.

Click!

"Good one," said the Traveller, as he got to his feet and started walking. The others got up and followed. The plane was a hundred metres away from them. The front wheel cover was down, but they could see the wheel itself still firmly in its place.

"The nose is still a bit high," said the Traveller. "We need it to be a bit lower. Get down in that ditch, and we'll give it a couple more seconds."

The group crouched down again, and the Traveller tapped Jake's arm.

Click!

The noise of the engines was unbelievable but, unlike Seeker, Splitter and Retro, Jake resisted the temptation to cover his ears. After a couple of seconds, the Traveller tapped his arm again.

Click!

Everything froze again, although the noise of the engines still rang in Jake's ears.

"Right, that should do it," said the Traveller. "Splitter, Jake, I'll need a step ladder. Can you get me one?" They looked at him.

"Where from?" asked Splitter, looking around him.

The Traveller looked around. "Over there," he said. "That building there looks like a maintenance shed. There should be one in there."

"Okay," said Splitter. "Jake, take my hand."

As soon as Jake had taken hold of Splitter's hand, Splitter clicked his fingers. They were instantly transported to the maintenance shed.

"Wow, cool," said Jake. "It must be great to be able to do that."

"Similar to your own power, I suppose. That must be pretty cool too."

"Yeah, but it took a bit of getting used to. It's a really weird feeling when everything else around you stops."

"You think that's weird," said Splitter. "Try doing this, and seeing yourself just over there. I can feel and hear everything in both places. Now *that's* weird!"

Jake laughed. "Yeah, it must be."

"Right, let's find this ladder," said Splitter as he looked around.

It didn't take them long. There was a tall, heavy stepladder in one corner. Jake tried to lift it, but couldn't.

"Don't worry about that," said Splitter. We don't need to carry it, just hold it. As long as we're holding hands too, we'll all go back to the others when I click."

"Of course," said Jake with obvious relief. He took hold of the ladder with one hand, and Splitter's hand with the other.

"Ready?" asked Splitter.

"Yup."

Splitter clicked his fingers, and they were back with the others. The duplicate version of Splitter had disappeared.

"Thanks, guys," said the Traveller. "Now, give me a hand to get this just under the front wheel."

They hauled the ladder over to the front of the plane, and opened it up. It was just high enough for the Traveller to reach the wheel. He took out a heavy duty screwdriver and put it between his teeth before climbing the ladder. He had a wrench in his back pocket.

After a few moments, he called down.

"I think I've found the problem. I shouldn't be much longer." He fiddled a bit longer and then said: "Okay, that should do the trick." He came down the ladder. "We'll have to move the ladder back a bit, so that the wheel doesn't hit it when I pull it down."

The ladder was repositioned, and the Traveller went up again. He pulled on the arm of the wheel. Nothing happened immediately, but after a few more hard tugs it began to move. Finally, it dropped down.

The Traveller checked it thoroughly. "It should automatically be locked into position now," he said.

He came down the ladder again.

"Right, let's fold this up. Everybody back into the ditch. We'll keep the ladder with us for the moment, in case the wheel isn't locked. Let's leave it here, and move up there a bit so that we can see if it works, otherwise the plane will be past us in a flash."

They moved up the runway towards the lights of the emergency vehicles, then jumped into the ditch and crouched down again. The Traveller tapped Jake's arm.

The deafening noise resumed instantly as the aircraft rushed towards them. They all held their breath as the nose of the plane came down. The front wheel touched the runway just in front of them, and remained locked in position. It didn't collapse.

The Traveller shouted "YES!" involuntarily, but the noise of the engines ensured that he would not have been heard beyond the small group crouching with him in the ditch. They watched the plane as it slowed and finally came to rest to be surrounded by the emergency vehicles. Jake wished he had a radio with him: he'd love to have listened to the conversation between the plane and the control tower as they realised that the wheel had come down just before the crash landing.

"Well done," he said to the Traveller.

"Thanks," he said. "Looks like it worked a treat. Hey, better stop time again so that we can go back."

Click!

"Good work, everybody. Right, let's link up, and Retro can take us back."

"What about the ladder?" asked Jake. "Shouldn't we put it back?"

"Good point. I forgot about that — that would have caused a bit of confusion, eh?" said the Traveller.

Jake and Splitter returned the stepladder to its original place in the maintenance shed, and then rejoined the others.

They linked arms and, when they were all ready, Retro clicked her fingers. Instantly, they were back in the white room where the Master was waiting for them.

"A successful mission, I gather?" he said as the group unlinked their arms and returned to their positions in the formal circle.

"Yes, Master," said the Traveller, "we did it. A disaster was avoided."

"You did it, you mean," said Splitter with a grin.

"No, no, we *all* did it," said the Traveller. "Sure, I pulled the wheel down, but it would have been impossible to do it on my own. You all had a vital role to play, so we all deserve the credit."

"That's exactly right," said the Master. "It was a fine team effort. Thanks to one and all. Is there any other business for us to discuss?"

"If I may, Master?" said the Traveller. The Master nodded, and the Traveller turned to Seeker.

"Seeker," said the Traveller, "how did it all turn out in the end?"

"Hang on a moment, and I'll go and find out for you," she said. She clicked her fingers and vanished, reappearing almost instantly, brandishing a newspaper. The headline read:

NARROW ESCAPE FOR 460 PASSENGERS ON "DOOMED" JET

"It says here that the front wheel of the plane malfunctioned, but dropped down on its own accord just after the rear wheels hit the surface of the runway. They think the vibration jolted the front wheel into dropping down. All 460 passengers escaped unharmed, although the pilot and several passengers were later treated for shock."

"Brilliant," said the Traveller. "Well, a good night's work, I think."

"Indeed," said the Master. "You all deserve to sleep well tonight. Thank you for all your efforts. We'll meet again soon, I trust." And he vanished.

The others were too tired to hang around, so they said their farewells and, one by one, disappeared to get some sleep.

CHAPTER THIRTEEN

Jake was exhilarated when, three weeks later, he read the full story in the newspaper. He knew how different the outcome could have been, and he felt proud to have played a part in saving the plane and its passengers. His happiness was tempered by the fact that he couldn't share it with anybody. Who would believe him anyway? Well, Fergus probably would, but it was inconceivable that Jake could tell him. No, it would have to be his secret. He had told Mr Walker of course, but nobody else could ever know the truth.

It was autumn now, and the warm sunny weather of late summer had been replaced by an almost constant drizzle. Leaves were falling from the trees in their thousands, most of them rotting where they fell, and the evenings seemed short and miserable. Everybody seemed to be fed up with such weather, and a sense of misery appeared to grip the nation.

Fergus had not been seen or heard of since Jake had spotted him crouching behind his car. He hadn't written any articles about the Timekeepers, and seemed to be keeping a low profile, although Jake was sure he hadn't given up. He was always on guard, checking to see if Fergus was following him to or from school, and looking out of the net curtains at home regularly to see if the battered old car was parked up the road.

Jake had been especially careful on the few occasions when he'd used his powers in the last three weeks. He'd just managed to stop somebody's car keys from falling down a drain, and he'd picked the pocket of a pickpocket who'd just stolen a wallet, returning it to the coat pocket of the victim who wasn't aware that anything had happened anyway. The one he was most proud of was saving a child who had fallen from the top of a climbing frame in the park. The child was heading for the ground head first, but Jake had swung him round so that he landed on his feet. He still fell over and grazed his knees on landing, but it could easily have been so much worse.

It was a Tuesday, and Jake was on his way home from school. As usual, he was listening to music on his portable CD player while he strolled unhurriedly along the High Street towards the park. All of a sudden, he saw Fergus leaning against a shop window just in front of him. It looked as if he was waiting for somebody. Jake was instantly alert.

"Jake!" he said with a broad grin. "Good to see you again."

Jake pulled the earphones from his ears and stopped. "Hello," he said politely. "Are you waiting for somebody?"

"Yes," said Fergus. "You, actually."

"What? I thought I told you not to follow me around."

"You did, yes. And I haven't been following you, have I? But it's obvious that you'll take this route to school from your house, and I thought I'd ask if you fancied another cup of tea and a chat."

"A chat? What about?" asked Jake cautiously.

"Oh, this and that," said Fergus.

"This and that?" repeated Jake.

"Look," said Fergus, "I think we might have got off to a bad start last time we met. That was my fault, I admit. I'm sorry about that. It's just that I tend to be a bit clumsy like that sometimes, especially if I'm preoccupied with the Ti – well, with my favourite subject."

Jake relaxed a bit, and smiled. "Some would call it an obsession," he said. He looked at his watch. It was still only four o'clock, and he had nothing better to do. Having a cup of tea with Fergus might provide the opportunity to find out what he was up to, although he'd have to keep on his guard. "Okay, why not?"

They went into a trendy café called The Chill Zone, where coffee was served in mugs and customers sat around in deep armchairs and on comfy sofas. Modern art paintings – the sort of things that children could easily produce – hung on the walls, and soft classical music provided a serene atmosphere. All of this was in contrast to most of the other cafés in the town, which only used hard metal chairs and formica-topped tables, often deafening their customers with blaring music from a variety of radio stations.

Fergus bought the tea, and took it to where Jake had settled into an armchair. He poured three teaspoons of sugar into his own mug, and began stirring furiously. By the time he had finished, there was froth on top of the tea. It looked repulsive, Jake thought, as he took a sip from his own mug.

"I'm curious," said Fergus as he sat down heavily on the edge of a sofa.

"About what?" asked Jake. It seemed to be a particular trick of Fergus, to get the other person to ask what he wanted to talk about. It was almost as if the ensuing conversation was not started by Fergus.

"Well, you know my views about Timekeepers, I think..."

"Oh, that again," groaned Jake.

"Now don't go getting angry again, please," said Fergus. "I'd like to have a civilised talk, not an argument. Is that really too much to ask?"

Jake sighed. "Alright, I'm listening."

"Look, I've been thinking things through over the past few weeks. I've looked at it from every conceivable angle. It's driving me crazy, you know – I'm hardly getting any sleep – but I just can't get it out of my head, this thing about Timekeepers. And I always reach the same conclusion."

"And what's that?" Jake asked, not feigning interest.

"Somehow – I don't know how – you have become a Timekeeper – "

"Now just a – " began Jake, but Fergus held up his hand to cut him off.

"Listen, please?" he begged. Jake sat back, saying nothing.

"It used to be Mr Walker – you know, the old boy who lives across the road from you – you two are close, I understand?"

"That's none of your business," said Jake.

"True, but you probably already know that he and I don't exactly get on. He took out a restraining order against me. He must have mentioned it, when you visited his house after our last meeting?"

"So you followed me," said Jake, holding his stare. He was tempted to say that he knew that Fergus had been there, but simply said, "I thought you might have done."

"Yes," said Fergus. "I'm not proud of it but, in a way, that's my job. I've spent half my life following people around, chasing a story. It's what I do, and sometimes it causes trouble for me, as you can imagine." He held Jake's stare. "Will you let me tell you what I know? I accused you of being a Timekeeper, and I'm sure you'd want to know how I reached that conclusion? I need to explain the background, and I'm sure you'll understand me better once you've heard me out. Humour me, won't you, if only for the sake of a free cup of tea?"

"Alright," said Jake. "I presume you'd keep pestering me anyway. As I said, I'd call the police if you did that, but I really don't want that sort of hassle – and I'm sure you could do without it too. So, I'll listen to what you've got to say, but then I'm going, okay?"

He saw a wave of relief flood over Fergus' features, and instantly felt sorry for him. He couldn't help wondering whether it would be possible – sensible, even – for the Timekeepers to consider doing a deal with Fergus, confirming the truth in exchange for Fergus' word that he would never publish a single detail of what he heard. At least that would put the poor man's mind at rest. But that level of responsibility was way, way above Jake's head. He'd need to think about it very carefully before he made any mention of the idea to the Traveller, let alone the Master. Once I've heard what Fergus has to say, he thought, I'll be in a better position to know what to do.

"Thank you," said Fergus. "Let me start from the beginning – as far as I know it. A few years back, I was searching through some old papers of mine. I found a document which I'd clearly written, but about which I had absolutely no recollection. As a journalist, of course, I can just about remember everything I've ever produced, or at least I'd recognise it if I saw it again. But this document was different. It was almost like the rudimentary plot for a novel I intended to write, but – "

"Do you have a copy of the document?" asked Jake.

"Oh, yes," said Fergus, eyeing Jake warily. "Yes, indeed. But it's in a very safe place, for reasons which I'll explain in due course."

"Sorry, I didn't mean to interrupt you."

"No problem. At least it shows you're listening to what I have to say, and for that I am grateful."

"Please, go on," prompted Jake.

"As I was saying, I've never had any intention of writing a book," said Fergus. "So it was truly confusing to find a document such as this. It started me thinking. When had I written it, and for what purpose? The information it contained at first seemed fanciful, and I was as sceptical about it as most people have been ever since, but I needed to get to the bottom of it. One piece of crucial information I had recorded was the name and address of one of the Timekeepers – Mr Walker – who, according to the document, was a close friend of mine. I checked it out, and found that Mr Walker really did exist, and lived at the address given, but of course I'd never even heard of him. Why, then, would I record the name and address of somebody I'd never met, and call him a close friend? The mystery deepened. So I went to see him, to see if he could shed any light on it."

"What happened?" asked Jake.

"Well, that's when things started getting really weird," continued Fergus. "As soon as Mr Walker opened the door and saw me standing there, he looked – I don't know – shocked. I saw it in his eyes, just a fleeting expression of amazement. It was almost as if I was a ghost or something. After a fraction of a second, he changed, but I know that there was a flash of recognition in his eyes when he first saw me. I've been a journalist for a long time, Jake, and it's a prime rule of journalistic interviews that you watch people's eyes. You can tell whether they're telling the truth, whether they're scared, hiding some crucial piece of information, or whatever."

It was an effort for Jake not to squirm in his seat as he realised that his own guilt must be glaringly obvious to Fergus. He picked up a paper serviette and pretended to blow his nose as he felt himself begin to blush. But Fergus seemed too wrapped up in telling his story — for the first time to a willing listener — to notice.

"So I concluded that there must have been some truth in the document I had written. As you know already, I followed Mr Walker around, trying to get evidence that something was going on, but it was impossible to catch him in the act, so to speak. I confronted him on a number of occasions, even pleaded with him to explain what was going on, but he refused to acknowledge me and, after a while, he took out a restraining order against me."

"So you said," said Jake.

"It was the most humiliating thing. My career went downhill — I almost had to build my credibility from scratch, and a number of so-called friends stopped speaking to me — but, by then, I was totally consumed by this whole issue. It had completely taken over my life. I couldn't think about anything else — I started drinking quite heavily, I put on weight, couldn't sleep — I've been a bit of a mess ever since. But despite all that, I *know* I'm right. I know it."

He looked at Jake, who had assumed a genuine expression of sympathy.

"And now you come into it," said Fergus.

"How do you mean," asked Jake.

"You're involved — somehow — aren't you?"

"Involved? How do you figure that? Look, I almost got run over by a bus and I live near Mr Walker, that's all," said Jake. "I've lived in the same road as him since I was born, and he's always been like a grandfather to me. We talk a lot, and he'll give me advice if I ask him for it. That hardly makes me a Timekeeper."

"You don't deny their existence, then?" said Fergus.

"Deny it? I don't know if they exist or not. You say they do, and everyone else says they don't. Why should I believe you instead of them? You even called me a Timekeeper."

"Is that such a bizarre concept?"

"I'm sixteen, for God's sake," said Jake hotly. "I like sleeping, and most of the time I have difficulty getting out of bed when the alarm clock goes off. I've got a cheap watch that goes about ten minutes fast every week – look!" He showed Fergus his rather plain watch. "Great Timekeeper I'd be!"

Fergus sighed heavily. He obviously wasn't going to get anything else out of Jake today.

"You know, Jake, I question myself every single day. I ask myself whether it's all a load of bullshit, whether I'm just going off my trolley. Maybe I suffered some sort of breakdown after I wrote that document – that might explain why I can't remember it – "

"Yeah, maybe," agreed Jake.

"– except it's the only thing in the whole of my life that I can't remember doing! I've got a good memory, I can remember way back to when I was a child. I can remember articles I wrote soon after leaving college, essays I wrote for my English 'A' level. So how can I have no recollection of that document? It doesn't make sense, does it?"

"No it doesn't," agreed Jake, "but then I'm only a teenager, aren't I? What would I know about long-term memory? I can't even remember what I wrote in my GCSE essays a few months ago. Maybe you should speak to a psychologist or something."

"Or a psychiatrist, you mean?"

"Maybe it'd help?"

"I don't think so," said Fergus. "No, I came to the conclusion a long time ago that I'm not mad." He smiled ruefully. "There are probably thousands of people out there who would disagree with that diagnosis, I'm sure. If I had any other reason – just one – to think that I had mental problems, I'd go and see a shrink straight away. But it all comes down to that one document, and my quest for the truth."

Jake pushed his teacup away and looked at his watch. "Well, Mr Dingley – "

"Please, Jake, please call me Fergus. There's no need for us to be so formal, is there?"

"Alright – Fergus," Jake said, "I'm not sure I can help you any more. I'd better be off."

"Perhaps we can meet again?" said Fergus.

"Why?"

"I don't know, really. As I said, you're different. At least you had the courtesy to listen to what I had to say. I still think you know more about all this than you're letting on…"

"I don't – "

Fergus held up his hand. "No, Jake, it's alright. If I'm right – and I'm afraid I'm still convinced that I am – then I am sure you have a good reason for being reticent with me."

"You still think I'm a Timekeeper?"

"Yes, but I wouldn't expect you to admit it. Mr Walker never did."

"Well, you're wrong."

"Am I?" said Fergus. "As I said to begin with, so many things just don't add up. If I'm wrong, then there must be another explanation for how you miraculously escaped from the path of that bus. I'm not a religious man, so I don't believe that a flock of angels swooped down and moved you. But I'm convinced that you know what happened and, as far as I can see, the only possible explanation is that you are a Timekeeper. According to all the witness statements, Mr Walker wasn't in the vicinity at the time, so either you've taken over his role, or perhaps you are both Timekeepers."

There was a moment's silence as the two looked at each other, each trying to determine what the other was thinking.

"You're not going to – "

"– Start following you around?" said Fergus. "No, you'd be expecting that, and I'm sure it wouldn't do either of us any good. No, I'd much rather have a chat with you every now and then, openly."

"I don't know," said Jake. He was unsure. If he declined, Fergus would probably resort to following him around, despite Jake's threat of calling the police. And if he agreed, Fergus might assume that he was right about Jake knowing more than he was prepared to say, but at least Jake could keep his colleagues informed of what Fergus was thinking and saying. Not much of a choice, thought Jake.

"Okay," he said as he stood up, "I don't know why you think I'd be able to help, but I'm prepared to have a cup of tea with you every now and then, if that's what you want."

Fergus grinned. Jake felt unnerved, and a little ashamed. Was Fergus really so lonely that he saw Jake as a friend? Is this what had become of Fergus, after years of trying to find out the truth about the Timekeepers? He felt sorry for the guy.

"I'll call you, then," said Fergus, still smiling, as Jake started to head for the door.

Jake looked over his shoulder. "Yeah, whatever," he said. Once out of sight of the café, he leant against a wall and took a deep breath. Like last time, he decided to go and talk it over with Mr Walker, and he'd call the Traveller later.

He set off towards the park. He looked back once, but he was sure Fergus wouldn't try to follow him this time. He probably knew that Jake would go straight to Mr Walker's house again, so there would be nothing to gain by confirming that.

Jake's mind was in turmoil as he walked slowly through the park, trying to disentangle his feelings. In a way, he liked Fergus: he certainly felt sorry for him. Jake's natural instinct would be to tell Fergus that he was right, so that he could free him from the mental anguish he was so clearly experiencing. But Jake knew that, however right it might be to do that, it could never be in the best interests of the Timekeepers for anybody else – and especially a journalist – to know their secret. Jake couldn't quite figure it all out but, for some reason, he couldn't help feeling utterly miserable.

CHAPTER FOURTEEN

Jake arrived at Mr Walker's house shortly after five o'clock. It was almost dark, and there was a slight drizzle which compounded Jake's feeling of misery. There were no lights on in the house, and the curtains in the front room had not been drawn. From the pavement, Jake could make out some of the furniture and the pictures which reflected the dim orange glow of the street lamp. Perhaps he's asleep, thought Jake as he walked around to the front door and rang the bell. It wasn't like Mr Walker to go out at this time of day. He normally went out every morning, if only for a walk, but he always liked to spend the afternoons and evenings at home, especially now the evenings were drawing in, and the weather was colder.

There was no answer.

Jake walked around to the front of the house, and cupped his hand to look in through the window. Mr Walker was lying on the floor, in the middle of the lounge, quite motionless.

Oh my God, thought Jake. He rapped on the window and called out, but Mr Walker's inert form showed no sign of response.

Jake looked up and down the street. There was nobody around to call for help. He went round to the back door and tried the handle. It was locked.

He took out his mobile phone, and dialled the emergency number.

"I need an ambulance – hurry! It's Mr Walker, he's – he's not moving."

"What address are you calling from?"

"Duckworth Close, number 11. Please, hurry!"

"Duckworth Close," repeated the operator, typing the road name onto her computer. "May I have your name, please, caller?"

"What – er, Jake. Jake Hepton. I live at number 23. The doors are locked and I can't get in, but I can see Mr Walker lying there. He's not moving."

"Alright, Jake," said the operator calmly. "An ambulance is on its way to you. Stay calm, it'll be with you in a few minutes."

"Thanks."

Jake rang off. His heart was thumping in his chest as he paced up and down. He went to the back door again, and tried to force it open, but the locks held firm. He couldn't stand it: he had to do something.

Then he had an idea.

Click!

He pulled out the pocket watch and stared at the dial. After only a moment's hesitation, he pushed down on the crown and turned half the minute hand round to the number ten. Then he released the crown.

In an instant, the Timekeepers all appeared around him. Seeker, Retro and Splitter were a bit disoriented, but Traveller was obviously used to being called upon at short notice.

"Jake, what's up?" he said.

"It's Mr Walker," said Jake. "He's lying on the floor inside. He's not moving, but I can't get in. He's not asleep, I'm sure – I hammered on the window and he didn't wake up."

"Where is he?"

"In the lounge – you can see him through the window at the front."

"Okay, let's have a look," said the Traveller. He ran round to the front, followed by the others, and looked through the window.

Seeker and Retro covered their mouths in shock when they saw Mr Walker on the floor.

"Have you called an ambulance?" asked Retro.

"Yes," said Jake. "It was on its way, but I had to do something, so I called everybody to come here."

"Good thing you did, Jake," said the Traveller. "Time's stopped, but we've got to get in. Splitter, give us a hand."

"Sure," said Splitter. "Link up, then." Everybody linked arms, and Splitter clicked his fingers. Instantly, they were standing in the lounge. Seeker flicked the light switch, and they all knelt down beside Mr Walker.

Retro took charge. "Come on, give him room, everyone." The circle widened a bit. Jake helped Retro turn Mr Walker onto his back. The body was limp and cool. Retro felt for a pulse, and listened for any signs of breathing. She looked up at the others, and slowly shook her head.

"No!" shouted Jake. "He's not – he's..."

"I'm sorry, Jake," said Retro. "He's gone."

"How – how can you be sure?"

"I'm a nurse, Jake," she said. "He's gone." She sighed. "It looks like he suffered a heart attack. There's no sign of any other trauma – besides, the doors are all locked from inside."

Tears welled up Jake's eyes and ran down his cheeks. Retro put her arm gently round his shoulders. Seeker was weeping silently, holding a handkerchief to her mouth, while Splitter tried to comfort her. The

Traveller stared down at Mr Walker, lost in thought. There was a period of silence. In their own way, and with their own memories, each of the Timekeepers said their own farewell to their former colleague.

"Retro," said Jake, "couldn't you – you know – take him back in time?"

"No, Jake," she said softly. "You know I can't do that."

"Why not?" He looked around for support from the others, but saw none.

"Jake," said the Traveller, "you know we can't interfere with the natural process."

"Yes, but…"

"And what would it achieve? We couldn't prevent Mr Walker from having a heart attack if we took him back. I'm sorry, Jake, but there's nothing we can do. I know you and he were close, but we have to let nature take its course, however hard it seems sometimes."

Jake looked at his colleagues through tear-filled eyes. "Yeah, you're right, I know. It just seems so unfair for his life to have ended like this. He must have been so lonely when he –"

"No, Jake," said Seeker quietly. "He might have been on his own when he died, but he was never lonely in his life. There's a difference, you know. And as far as I could see, it was you who made that difference for him. You meant the world to him."

"Yeah, that's right," said Splitter. "And besides, he'd have hated anybody to actually see him drop down dead – especially you, Jake. You'd probably have felt guilty for the rest of your life that you weren't able to save him, and that's the last thing he'd have wanted – well, you know what I mean…"

Despite the circumstances, Jake managed a weak smile at Splitter's unfortunate wording. He sniffed, and wiped his eyes with his forearm. "Yeah, I s'pose," he said, not altogether convinced.

The Traveller stood up slowly, still looking solemnly down at Mr Walker's body.

"I have to inform the Master," he said. "He'll want to know what's happened." He clicked his fingers and disappeared, returning almost instantly with the Master. The other Timekeepers stood up instinctively, and moved back to give the Master some space.

The Master knelt down beside Mr Walker and touched his face gently with the back of his fingers. The others stood in silence.

The Master spoke to Mr Walker. "Your time has come, my son. You served me well for many years, and for that you have my eternal gratitude. Sleep well, dear friend."

Jake let out an involuntary sob. The Master stood up, and rested a hand lightly on Jake's shoulder.

"Mortality," he said. "I shall never understand it. How much pain it causes." He shook his head. "But Mr Walker had a long and wonderful life, one which he enjoyed to the full. I knew him for many years, and he was one of the best, most vibrant, men I ever met. There was no sadness in him, nor malice. It is right that we should grieve for him at the time of his passing, but he would not have wanted us to grieve for long. He was not like that. I am sure he would want us to celebrate his life, rather than mourn his death. It comforts me, at least, to know that he would not have suffered."

The Master turned to Jake. "I should like to attend his funeral, in order to pay my last respects to a man whom I was proud to call a friend. I suspect we would all want to attend." There was a murmur of agreement from the others. "Jake, perhaps you could contact the Traveller at an appropriate point during the service, and we shall come."

Jake found some inner strength, and wiped his eyes again.

"Of course, Master," he said. "I know Mr Walker would want you all to be there."

"That's settled, then," said the Master. "In the meantime, remind yourself regularly of the pure goodness of the man. You should smile when you think of him. He'd like that."

Jake nodded. The Master patted his shoulder gently, and disappeared.

"Right, come on everyone," said the Traveller. "We, too, must leave so that the natural course of events can continue. The ambulance crew will take good care of Mr Walker."

"Wait," said Jake. "Before we go, let's open one of the top windows there."

"Why do that?" asked the Traveller.

"I can't bear the thought of them having to break into the house," said Jake. "I told them I couldn't get in, but if we leave the top window open, they can open the main window. At least they wouldn't need to break the door down to get in."

"Fair enough," said the Traveller. He looked up and down the road. "Nobody's going to notice that – there's no-one around anyway."

94

Jake opened a top window, and put it on the latch so that the ambulance crew would be able to open another window and climb in.

"Right, let's go," said Splitter. They linked arms, and Splitter took them back outside the house.

Seeker and Retro both hugged Jake hard, and Retro gave him a kiss on the cheek.

"Be brave," she said.

"Thanks," said Jake. He shook hands with the Traveller and Splitter. "Thanks for being here."

"You didn't exactly give us much choice!" said Splitter.

"No," said Jake, "but I hope you didn't mind."

"Mind?" said the Traveller. "I'd have been very upset if you hadn't called us. You did exactly the right thing."

He punched Jake lightly on the arm. "Take care of yourself, hey?"

"Yeah, I'll try."

He took out his pocket watch, pressed down on the crown, and reunited the two halves of the minute hand.

"Thanks again," he said. He let go of the crown, and they all vanished.

The immediate silence was eerie. He stood there for a few moments, reflecting on the strong bond which existed between the Timekeepers. It gave him strength and comfort, and he took a deep breath.

Click!

The resumption of normality was hardly noticeable. Nothing moved, and there was only a faint whisper of traffic as it passed by the end of the road. After a couple of minutes, Jake heard the distant siren of the ambulance. The noise grew louder as it approached.

As the ambulance turned into Duckworth Close, Jake ran to the front gate and waved his arms above his head. He realised that, although he now felt calm and in control, he needed to act as distressed as he had been on the phone only a few minutes earlier. He knew there was nothing they could do, but he had to pretend that there was still hope. It was hard, but it had to be done.

"Quick!" he shouted as the ambulance drew up outside the house. "In here!"

The ambulance crew grabbed some medical equipment from the back of the vehicle, and came over to join Jake. A couple of neighbours, alarmed at the sound of ambulance sirens in their street, also came out of their houses and started towards Mr Walker's house.

The paramedic peered in through the front window, and saw Mr Walker.

"You've tried the doors?" he asked Jake.

"Yes, they're locked, back and front," he said.

The paramedic looked around. "Here," he said, "there's a window open there. I'll see if I can reach in to open the main window."

Good, thought Jake, just as I had hoped.

The paramedic worked quickly, and climbed through the main window, followed by his colleague. Jake climbed in too, but stayed by the window as the paramedic set to work. He did the same checks as Retro had done. Jake knew that the result would be the same, but he couldn't help hoping that perhaps Retro had got it wrong.

The paramedic looked up at Jake and shook his head. "He's dead," he said.

Jake looked away. Hearing it put so bluntly was enough to remove any pretence at grief, and his shoulders shook as he cried once again. Mr Walker had been more than a friend to him. He had been a soulmate, a colleague, a tutor, an advisor, all rolled into one. To lose all of that so suddenly was, for Jake, devastating. He felt empty, numb, as if his entire world had just collapsed around him. He walked slowly past the paramedic and out of the room into the hallway. He opened the front door and walked outside, as if in a trance.

A small crowd of neighbours had gathered in the front garden, watching the paramedic through the window. Most of them had lived in Duckworth Close for as long as Jake could remember: Mr Sinclair, Mr and Mrs Cuthbertson, Colonel Hythe-Blunkett, Mrs Wallis, and Professor Denton. There was silence as they watched Jake approach. They had all known the special bond between Mr Walker and Jake, and their sympathy was almost overpowering.

"He's dead," whispered Jake, almost to himself. He walked towards the front gate, and the group opened a path for him, patting him on the shoulder or murmuring soft words of condolence as he passed.

He crossed the road and let himself into his own house. He could hear Alice listening to music upstairs in her bedroom, evidently oblivious to the events outside in the street. Jake went into the front room and looked out of the net curtains in time to see the ambulance crew carrying a stretcher from Mr Walker's house. They walked through the small group of neighbours, most of whom bowed their heads in respect – the more religious ones crossed themselves – , and put the stretcher in the back of the ambulance.

A police car drew up, and the policeman spoke briefly to the paramedic, who pointed at Jake's house. The policeman went into Mr Walker's house, secured the front windows and, after a few minutes, came back out.

Jake let the net curtain drop, and went upstairs with a heavy heart to break the sad news to Alice.

Supper in the Hepton household was a subdued affair that evening. Jake's parents had come home from work to find a policeman talking to Jake about how he had discovered the body of Mr Walker. Alice had been sitting on the sofa next to Jake, bursting into tears every time Jake had to repeat the story.

The policeman had concluded that there had been no foul play. The paramedic had said that Mr Walker had probably died of a massive heart attack, and that an autopsy would likely confirm the fact. There would be no further investigations. On searching the house, the policeman had discovered details of Mr Walker's solicitor, and the police would inform him. There seemed to be no other next of kin.

Jake still felt dazed, as if it was all part of a bad dream. When recounting what he done in the minutes after discovering the body, he had to take extra care not to mention contacting anybody else.

After the policeman had finally left, Jake's mother sat between him and Alice on the sofa, an arm around each of them as she consoled her children. Jake's father ordered a take-away from the local Chinese, so that his wife wouldn't need to cook dinner. They sat there eating, none of them feeling in the slightest bit hungry.

After a particularly long silence, Jake's father suggested that they each recount one happy memory that they had shared with Mr Walker, either as a family or individually. This seemed to help enormously and, once the ball was rolling, they were all smiling and laughing at each other's tales. Jake seemed to have so many tales to tell but, all the while, he found it hard to ignore the biggest tale of all. No, he decided, I owe it to Mr Walker's memory to maintain the secret, even within my own family.

It was difficult for any of them to get to sleep that night. Jake lay awake, wondering how different his life would be from now on. He had lost a close friend, the only person in his immediate vicinity with whom he could discuss the Timekeepers, and the person who had trusted him sufficiently to make him one. He felt alone and vulnerable, and wondered what the future would bring.

CHAPTER FIFTEEN

With the help of some of the other Duckworth Close residents, Jake's father took on the responsibility for organising Mr Walker's funeral. The solicitor had confirmed that there was no other known living relative.

The autopsy had been held, confirming the suspicions of the paramedic that Mr Walker's death had been caused by a massive coronary. The body had been released from the morgue and the undertakers were making the final preparations for the funeral to take place at a local church in a couple of days time.

It was Thursday, a week since Jake had made his distressing discovery on the way home from meeting Fergus. The solicitor had arranged a meeting for that evening to read the last will and testament of Mr Walker, which had been deposited with him a few months earlier.

Jake had spent much of the last week in a state of shock, trying to come to terms with a tragedy that was more personal to him than he could tell his family. He had had no contact with the Timekeepers, and had not even used his powers once. On the way to and from school, he had been lost in his own thoughts, looking down at the ground as he walked, and therefore took no notice of what was happening around him.

The meeting was scheduled to take place at Jake's house at seven o'clock. The solicitor arrived a few minutes early, followed shortly afterwards by half a dozen neighbours from Duckworth Close. Jake's mum offered each of them a drink and, when they were all seated, the solicitor called the small meeting to order. He was a rather small, thin man with neatly trimmed grey hair. He was smartly dressed in a dark suit, with a pressed white handkerchief in the top pocket of his jacket. He took out a pair of half-moon spectacles, perching them on the end of his slightly crooked nose, and peered around the room at his audience.

"As many of you may know," he said, "Mr Ronald Walker lived on his own. He died last Thursday in the house over the road which he had occupied for more than forty years. I had the good fortune to know him quite well, having acted for him on several occasions, and I should therefore like to take this opportunity to express my own sadness at his parting. He was, I think, the epitome of a gentleman." Around the room, there was a whispered chorus of agreement. The solicitor cleared his throat and waited for silence before continuing.

"In July this year, Mr Walker deposited with me his last will and testament, replacing an earlier version which was subsequently destroyed in his presence. In depositing his will, Mr Walker confirmed to me that he had no other living relative, and he therefore invited me to act as the executor of his estate. In the days since his death, I have undertaken the necessary research to determine the state of Mr Walker's financial affairs and assets. In this envelope," he said, holding it up for all to see, "I have the instructions given to me by Mr Walker for the management and distribution of those assets."

The solicitor ripped open the envelope, and pulled out the document within. He opened it and studied it for a minute in silence. At one point, Jake saw one of his eyebrows briefly rise and fall, but his expression was otherwise completely impassive. The audience watched him intently, waiting.

"Mr Walker lived a modest life, and his estate is not considerably large. It consists mainly of his house and its contents. There is a current account and a savings account, containing a total of about £4000. Mr Walker has requested, subject to the agreement of the residents of Duckworth Close, that a small garden be constructed in his memory at the end of the Close, on the small communal piece of land which leads to the fields. He has provided a draft plan of the garden, which includes a small pond and a clock tower – as many of you will know, he had something of a fascination with time."

Jake looked around the room, and saw several people nodding their agreement.

The solicitor went on. "Such a plan is of course subject to any local authority regulations and the agreement of residents. It would not of course have been Mr Walker's wish to cause any difficulties among the residents of Duckworth Close. Personally, though – and although I am not a resident myself – I think it is a splendid idea, worthy of your consideration. I will make copies of the plan and circulate them to all residents. If all are agreed, I could make all the necessary arrangements on your behalf, in my capacity as executor of Mr Walker's estate.

"I turn now to Mr Walker's property and other assets." He turned the page. "It was Mr Walker's wish that the residents of Duckworth Close be offered any of the contents of the property that they might wish to keep, in his memory. I will draw up a complete inventory, but the list includes such items as paintings, clocks and memorabilia acquired throughout his long life. He expressed a preference for his assets to go to good homes, where his friends in Duckworth Close can appreciate them. Once I have circulated an inventory, I suggest that I supervise a process of sealed bids. If more than one resident desires a particular item, I can consider the most appropriate course of action. Any items not retained by the residents of Duckworth Close shall be auctioned, with the proceeds going to – " he looked down at the document " – a suitable charity concerned with poverty reduction in Africa.

"And finally," he said, looking around the room, "we come to the matter of Mr Walker's house. He says that he gave this matter the deepest consideration. He has instructed me to retain the property, and to place it in trust. The ownership will then pass, on his twenty-first birthday, to Jake Hepton."

There was an audible gasp around the room. Jake's jaw dropped open, and he stared at the solicitor in amazement. Everybody turned to look at Jake, finding him just as stunned as everyone else in the room. Several people started whispering at once, although Jake couldn't make out what any of them were saying.

The solicitor peered over his half-moon glasses at Jake.

"You must be Jake, then?" he asked.

"Er – y-yes," he stammered.

"Then I would say that you're an extremely fortunate young man," said the solicitor.

Jake looked around the room. His parents and Alice were staring at him, dumbfounded.

"Why on earth would Mr Walker have left his house to you?" his father asked.

"Well, I knew he was always very fond of you, dear," his mother said, "but this – this is incredible."

Jake didn't know what to say. He knew that he had always been a favourite of Mr Walker – all the other residents had seen it, too. He'd expected, eventually, to be left a couple of his favourite paintings, but the house? It didn't make sense. Then again, very little in Jake's life had made sense since he had become a Timekeeper.

"Oh, there's one other thing," said the solicitor, interrupting Jake's thoughts. "Mr Walker left with me a personal note to pass on to you. He asked that you read the note in my office, and that you destroy it afterwards. Perhaps, in that note, you will find some explanation for his huge generosity."

"A personal note that you must read and destroy?" said his father. "What on earth is all that about?"

Even though Jake could not even guess what the note might say, he knew perfectly well that it would concern the Timekeepers. Why else would Mr Walker have gone to the trouble to ensure that Jake read the note privately, and to ensure that it was destroyed immediately?

For now, though, he had to try and stop his family, and the other residents, from being too curious about the contents of the note.

"He's just left me his house, Dad," Jake said. "I don't know why he did that, but I'm sure the note will explain it."

"I hope so," said his father, "because it doesn't make sense to me."

The day of the funeral arrived. There weren't many people at the church – mostly other Duckworth Close residents. Mr Walker didn't seem to have had any friends from further afield.

Fergus was there too. Jake had called him and invited him. After all, even though Fergus didn't know it, he had once been a good friend of Mr Walker's, and Jake felt sure that he'd have wanted him there. The restraining order hardly mattered now anyway, Jake thought.

It was a simple ceremony. The coffin was then carried outside into the graveyard where a new plot had been prepared. The priest said a few words, and the coffin was ready to be lowered into the ground.

Click!

Jake took out the pocket watch and turned half of the minute hand round to the number ten. It wasn't an emergency, he knew, but the other Timekeepers had all said they wanted to attend. He released the crown, and they all appeared, standing in a small group beside Jake. After a few seconds, the Master appeared as well. He was dressed in a pristine white cloak with a large hood that covered his features.

The Master pushed back his hood and stepped forward. He placed his hand gently on the coffin and whispered a final farewell to his friend. It was a touching scene, Jake thought. The Master obviously had more respect for Mr Walker than any of the other mourners who stood frozen at the graveside but, ironically, he could play no part in the funeral proceedings. By rights, he should have been able to stand in the pulpit of the church and tell people just how special Mr Walker had been, and how he had done so much, throughout his life, for the benefit of others. It was sad, but Jake knew that Mr Walker could never be given the full recognition he deserved. His secrets would have to be buried with him.

The other Timekeepers stood in silence with their heads bowed, paying their last respects to a friend and colleague. After a few minutes, the Master turned to Jake.

"Thank you, Jake," he said. "It was an honour for me to be present."

"I'm glad you could come, too," said Jake. "All of you. It would have meant a lot to Mr Walker that his closest friends were all able to attend."

The Master gave a sad smile and sighed. "We experienced so much together over the years. It's a drawback of immortality, you know, when you realise that your closest friends are always going to die before you. It's one of the sad certainties of my existence."

Jake thought it might be a long time before he had a better chance to learn more.

"Master, can I ask you something?"

"Of course, Jake, of course."

"How old are you – if it's not a rude question?"

The Master chuckled. "You know, Mr Walker asked me exactly the same question when he was young. But I'm afraid I couldn't give him an answer either. You see, I simply don't know."

"You don't know how old you are?" asked Jake.

"I'm sure that sounds odd to you, but no, I don't," said the Master. "You see, I don't measure my age in the same way as others do, by years. For me, time is constant, so years mean nothing to me as far as my personal age is concerned." He saw the look on Jake's face and smiled. "It certainly isn't meant to sound condescending, but I'm afraid that my concept of time is quite beyond human comprehension. Every living thing has a different concept of time. Some insects live for less than a day, while tortoises might live for a hundred years or more, and you couldn't expect the insect to understand the tortoise's concept of time. Using the same analogy, one might say that humans are like insects and I am like a tortoise. Does that make any sense?"

"Er – a little, I guess," said Jake.

The Master looked round the small group. They had all been listening, and all looked as pensive, and as confused, as Jake.

"I must go," he said. He patted Jake's shoulder. "Try not to grieve too long, Jake. You'll be fine, I promise." He pulled the large hood over his head, stood back from the group, and vanished.

"It's probably time for us to be going too, Jake," said the Traveller. "We mustn't overstay our welcome."

"Thanks again for being here," replied Jake.

102

He reunited the two halves of the minute hand on his pocket watch, and his colleagues instantly disappeared, each to their own lives.

Jake sighed, and lightly touched Mr Walker's coffin for the last time.

"Thanks for everything you did for me," he said quietly. "I'll never forget you. You were the nicest person I ever met. I just wish I could have told you that before you died."

"Then your wish has come true."

Jake was startled at the voice behind him. He spun round and saw Mr Walker standing a few feet away.

"Wha – how did – but you're – ?" he spluttered.

"Dead?" said Mr Walker. "Well, yes and no, Jake."

Jake's eyes were wide with fear and amazement. "What – what do you mean?"

Mr Walker took a step towards him, and Jake instinctively stepped back, on to the very edge of the grave.

"Calm down, Jakey, it's alright."

Nobody else had ever called him Jakey. It was like a slap in the face.

"My God," he breathed, "it *is* you...."

"Yes," said Mr Walker, "it is me."

With a loud sob, Jake ran to him and threw his arms around him. Mr Walker held him tight, embracing him with as much love as if he had been his own son. He stroked the back of Jake's head, and tears rolled down his face. They held each other in silence for a few minutes, neither wanting to let go. Eventually, Mr Walker put his hands on Jake's shoulders and gently pushed him back, holding him at arm's length. He took a handkerchief from the breast pocket of his jacket and held it out to Jake, who looked down at it, and then took it and wiped his eyes.

"I – I don't understand," he said. "What's happening?"

"A final gift to me from the Master," said Mr Walker, smiling. "Probably the finest gift anybody has ever given me."

"How do you mean?" asked Jake, more confused than ever. "Do you mean you're alive?"

"Well, as you can see, I'm very much alive – but just for now."

He saw that Jake still hadn't grasped it. The shock had probably been too much for him.

"Let me explain," said Mr Walker. "I knew my time was almost up. I've been ill for a few months now – obviously." He chuckled, nodding at his own coffin. "I'd always wanted to make you the Freezer – you were the natural choice for it – and, when I discovered that I had only a few months left to live, I arranged it with the Master. Only he was aware of the real reason that I wanted to quit – the others simply presumed that I was getting too old for the job but, if truth be told, I'd have carried on for a while longer."

"You knew you were dying?" asked Jake. "Why didn't you say something?"

"There wasn't much to say, Jakey. What would have been the point of telling you that I was about to die. You couldn't have done anything – nobody could – and you'd have spent all your time worrying about me instead of focussing on your school work. No, it was best that you didn't know."

"So – how come you're here now?"

"As I said, it was a final gift from the Master. I didn't know when I'd die, but I assumed that you'd probably find out before anyone else, if it happened at home. So I wrote my will, and put all my affairs in order. Before I relinquished my position as Freezer, I asked the Master if I could – just this once – go forward in time to see you at my funeral. You see, we had unfinished business, you and I."

"We did?"

"Yes. You know, like you said to me – in that box – a few minutes ago, I too wanted you to know that you were like the son I never had. I've loved every moment of the time we've spent together, from the minute you were born. Even if it sounds a bit conceited to say it, I know you will feel so lonely after my death – "

"*Will...?*"

"I'm sorry – I keep forgetting that I should be speaking in the past tense, even though for me it's the future. It is all rather confusing, I have to say!"

"You seem to be quite, I don't know, relaxed about it all," said Jake.

"To tell you the truth, I am. I've had a good life, and I don't have any regrets. I know I don't have long to live, and everything is in order. I've even managed to say farewell to the one person who has made the last few years of my life so happy. Besides," he chuckled, "it's not every day that a man can attend his own funeral in the future." He looked around at the mourners gathered at the graveside.

"My goodness, I see you invited Fergus."

"Well, he was a good friend of yours – even though he didn't know it. I thought you'd like him to be here."

"That's very thoughtful of you, Jakey. Goodness, they all look so sad, don't they?"

"They are — *we* are," said Jake. "Everybody thought the world of you. Besides, it seemed a bit sudden, your death. God, that sounds weird, standing here talking to you about it."

There was a moment of silence.

"Well, I'm afraid I must be getting back," said Mr Walker. Neither of them wanted this final meeting to end, but both were aware that it had to.

"Do you have to go?" asked Jake, desperately.

Mr Walker patted him on the shoulder. "You know I do, Jake," he said quietly. "I've done what I came to do." His face brightened a little. "Besides, you're due to come and see me soon, when you get home from school. At least I get to see you again, even if that meeting is now in the past for you."

Jake smiled. "Next time I see the Master, I'll thank him for allowing you to do this. And I promise I'll be strong."

"I know you will, Jakey, I know you will." He held out his arms. "Come."

Jake hugged him so hard that Mr Walker winced.

"Thanks again, for everything," he said.

"Look after yourself, Jakey."

"I will."

Reluctantly, they parted. Jake's eyes brimmed with tears, but he didn't want to cry. He had promised to be strong. Mr Walker nodded at the coffin.

"When that box goes into the ground," he said, "you'll know that I am perfectly at peace. So there's no reason for you to be sad any more."

"Don't worry, Mr Walker. This visit has made all the difference in the world to me."

Mr Walker smiled warmly at him. "Good bye then, Jakey."

"Good bye, Mr Walker."

Mr Walker vanished. Jake looked around him, wondering if it had all been some kind of bizarre dream, a final psychological response to Mr Walker's death. Then he realised that he was still holding the handkerchief that Mr Walker had given him to wipe his eyes. It was the proof he needed, and he smiled to himself. He pushed the handkerchief into his pocket and got back into position to restart time. It had been so long that he'd almost forgotten where he had been standing, but he found the place. He didn't care if it wasn't exactly right. All eyes were fixed on the coffin anyway, so it was unlikely that anybody would notice.

Click!

The service resumed, and the coffin was lowered into the ground. Jake felt a warm glow. Mr Walker was indeed at peace and, for the first time in the last ten days, so was Jake.

Once the ceremony was over, the mourners drifted away from the graveside, leaving the gravediggers to fill in the rest of the hole. As Jake walked back towards the car, he felt a tug on his sleeve. It was Fergus.

"Hi," said Jake. He sounded exhausted, drained. "Thanks for coming."

"No problem," said Fergus. "You know, I wasn't sure why you invited me, but I'm glad I came. Mr Walker and I had our differences, but I still had a lot of respect for him. He was a good bloke."

"Yes, he was."

Fergus hesitated. "Rumour has it that he left you his house."

Word gets around quickly, Jake thought. Fergus must have been digging for information from the Duckworth Close residents. He didn't look at Fergus. He just kept walking, with his head down. "And?"

"I mean, he must have thought very highly of you."

"You wouldn't understand. He was probably my best friend. One of the family."

"But his house? That's a pretty astonishing bequest to someone of your age."

"Is it really any of your business what Mr Walker did with his property?"

"Not really, I suppose. But it adds weight to the theory."

Jake stopped and turned to look directly at Fergus. "What?"

"It's not the only gift he gave you, is it? He made you a Timekeeper too, didn't he? Mr Walker conferred his powers to you, and even left you his house. What is it, a Timekeeper's residence?"

"This is a funeral," said Jake. "I'm not going to have another conversation with you about Timekeepers – especially not today." He strode off, leaving Fergus standing on his own.

"I'm not giving up, you know," Fergus called after him. "I'm going to prove it. I'll prove it if it's the last thing I do."

Jake rejoined his family in the car park and returned home. His mother had organised a small party for the residents of Duckworth

106

Close. Mr Walker had left some money for precisely that purpose. His father made a short, light-hearted speech, and they all lifted their glasses to the memory of a good friend.

Jake hadn't invited Fergus back for the party, and he was relieved. It sounded like Fergus was gearing up to be a nuisance again, but Jake was too tired to think about that particular problem now. The last of the Duckworth Close residents left at nine o'clock, and Jake went up to his bedroom shortly afterwards. He collapsed on the bed, fully dressed, and was soon in a deep, dreamless sleep.

CHAPTER SIXTEEN

Although it was Sunday, the solicitor had offered to open up his office so that Jake could read the letter from Mr Walker. With school, it would be difficult for Jake to go there during normal business hours on Monday.

His father had offered to drive him there but, since it was just the other end of the High Street, close to the school, Jake said he'd prefer to walk through the park. It was windy and drizzling with rain, but that hardly mattered to Jake. For the first time since Mr Walker's death, he felt relaxed and happy. He wondered how miserable he would have felt if Mr Walker had not been able to visit him at the graveside.

He met the solicitor outside the office, right on time, and followed him inside. The office was organised and tidy, but stuffed with neatly stacked files and bundles of paper bound up with ribbon.

The solicitor opened his safe, took out a plain white envelope and handed it to Jake. Jake saw that it was addressed simply to "Mr Jake Hepton" with, in the top left hand corner, the words "*Strictly private and confidential*". There was a wax seal on the back, with Mr Walker's initials either side of it.

"Have a seat," said the solicitor. "I'll leave you alone while you read it. I'll only be in the office next door, if you need me. Do you want a coffee or anything?"

"Just some water, please," said Jake.

"No problem." The solicitor went out and returned a minute later with a plastic cup of cold water. He set it on the table next to Jake. "I'll be next door, then."

"Thanks," said Jake. The solicitor went out of the room. Jake looked at the envelope for a moment, and ran his fingers over the wax seal, imagining Mr Walker sealing the letter.

He looked around, and found a letter opener on the solicitor's desk. He picked it up and inserted it under the corner flap of the envelope, and ripped it open.

The letter was two pages long. It was undated, but neatly handwritten in Mr Walker's own distinctive style. Jake had always thought that Mr Walker's handwriting was the best he had ever seen.

He started reading.

My dear Jake

I trust that my solicitor followed my instructions, and that you are now reading this letter in the privacy of his office. I'm sure you understand why I asked you to read this letter in private, and to destroy it as soon as you have read it, since I will make mention later of the Timekeepers.

I am sure that you were as surprised as everyone else when it was announced that I had bequeathed to you my house. The reason for that was, for me, simple. There was nobody else in the world that I would rather have left it to. I was never attracted to any particular charity, and it seemed quite wrong for me to leave it to the State.

I have special memories of our friendship during the last few years of my life, and it therefore seemed quite natural that I should repay you in a way that would make your own life more comfortable. The young people of today face so many challenges – many more than they did during my own youth – and it will make an old, if already departed, man very happy to think that he has been able to do something to reduce the challenges that you will inevitably face as you embark on the difficult journey into adult life.

The secrecy in which you read this letter is similar to the secrecy surrounding the Timekeepers. As you know, that was a secret I kept from you for many years, until I was confident that you were mature enough to assume the role of Freezer. But there is one other secret which, I am ashamed to admit, I was never able to reveal to you, and which represents the true reason for my bequest. We talked about many things, you and I, but there was one subject that we were never able to discuss. Now that I am dead, I can at last feel no guilt in revealing to you that secret. I am your grandfather.

Jake jolted upright. *I am your grandfather.* He stared at the sentence, dumbstruck. He read it three times, each time wondering whether he had misread it. He knew he should go on to the next paragraph, but his eyes couldn't be drawn away from the words *I am your grandfather.*

I've already got two grandfathers, thought Jake, but he knew instinctively that it was true. Mr Walker had never lied to him.

It was an effort, but he read on.

I am so sorry that those words will have been a shock to you – and even more sorry that I was unable to tell you them in person. When I said I had no regrets about my life, I was not wholly truthful. I had only one painful regret – that I would never be able to acknowledge you as my grandson for as long as I lived. But you deserve to know the truth and, now that I am dead, I have no hesitation in breaking my vow of silence to reveal something you should have been told many years ago.

In 1961, I met and fell in love with a wonderful woman. I was several years older than her, and I had just returned from many years travelling in Africa. We were destined to be married, but our proposed liaison did not receive the support of her parents. They saw me as a fanciful wanderer, without a job and with few prospects for earning a decent living. Artists, as I once told you, rarely become rich, and her parents could not countenance their daughter marrying a man whose attitude towards life was so carefree. She was taken away to the country, and within weeks was married to a more suitable bachelor – your grandfather as you know him to be. I was heartbroken, although I was consoled to some degree by the fact that her new husband was a kind and generous man who loved her as completely as she deserved to be loved.

Some months later, my former fiancée sent me a brief message to say that she had given birth to a daughter and that I was the natural father. She could not acknowledge the fact to anybody else – of course, her parents and husband knew the truth – but she could not bear to live with the guilt of me never knowing the truth. In those days, there was no question of her leaving her husband and returning to me. It was something that one had to accept, in order to save embarrassment and humiliation. Oh, how I wish it had been otherwise!

I followed my daughter's life from a distance – being a Timekeeper helped – but I could never have any formal contact with her. She married and moved here into Duckworth Close, and I took the first opportunity that arose to buy a house in the same road. Although I could never be acknowledged as her father, it gave me so much pleasure to live so close to her, and to watch her life develop. It was for that reason, you understand, that I have always taken a special interest in you. Alice was also as important to me, but it was you who I wanted to succeed me as Freezer.

As far as I am aware, your mother knows nothing of all this. I am sure that her parents did not tell her, and I see no reason for her to know now. It may therefore seem very selfish of me to break this news to you, especially when I had not done so in person, and for that I beg your forgiveness. If you do, however, decide in time to reveal the truth, my solicitor has been entrusted to hold various papers of mine, including the letter I received from your grandmother following the birth of your mother. Now that I am gone, I must leave it to you to decide whether such a revelation would cause nothing but distress, in which case I am content for it to remain, like the Timekeepers, our own secret.

I hope now that the reason for the secrecy of this letter, and for my bequest, are clear to you.

Remember, Jakey, always to live your life to the full, and never to waste an opportunity that presents itself to you. When you take over the ownership of the house, do please hold a small celebration with your fellow Timekeepers in memory of me. I would like that.

Well, my dear Jake, it only remains for me to wish you health and happiness for many years to come. I hope that, one day, in some other place, we might meet again.

With much love,
Your Grandfather

Jake read the letter three times over. He wanted to keep the letter so that he could read it often, but he knew that he would have to destroy it. The contents of the letter could never be shared with another living soul. He tried to memorise every sentence of it, but realised that would be futile. Besides, he couldn't concentrate. His head was swirling with a mixture of emotions: he felt relieved, happy, confused, sad, lonely and exhausted all at the same time. He knew it would take some time to make sense of it all but, in a way, the letter had clarified so much for him. Would he tell his mother? No, he decided. What good would it do? And how could something as momentous as that bring anything other than bitterness and regret to a family that was otherwise so close and happy? He'd like to tell Alice in due course, but perhaps he'd leave it a few years until they were both much older and wiser.

There was a knock on the door, followed by the muffled voice of the solicitor.

"Are you alright in there, Jake?"

"Er – yes, fine thanks."

"May I come in?"

"Sorry, yes of course."

The door opened and the solicitor studied Jake's face.

"My goodness, you look as if you've been through the mill. Not bad news, is it? I don't mean to pry, of course."

"That's okay. No, it's not bad news really. In fact, in many ways it's very good news, I think." The solicitor looked confused. "Now, I need to destroy the letter as Mr Walker had instructed."

"Yes, yes, of course. If you're ready to do that now, then?"

"Yes, I think so."

"Fine. Come this way. There's a shredding machine next door."

Jake followed him into the next office, where the solicitor switched on the machine. Jake stepped forward and held the letter over the shredder blades which rumbled loudly like an empty stomach waiting to be fed.

He looked at the letter for the last time, and slowly fed the two sheets of paper into the machine. White sawdust dropped from the bottom of the machine into a waste bin full of other shredded documents, and it was done. That's it, thought Jake. No evidence, nothing on paper. He stood looking at the white sawdust for a moment, until the solicitor coughed behind him.

"Oh, sorry," said Jake. "I was lost in thought for a minute."

The solicitor turned off the machine and motioned for Jake to leave the room.

"Are you sure you're alright?" he asked. "Shall I call your father and ask him to come and pick you up?"

"No," said Jake quickly. "No, honestly, I'm fine. I'll walk home, it's not far."

"If you're sure…"

"Thanks, I'm sure."

The solicitor let him out into the High Street. Jake shook his hand.

"Thanks for opening up on a Sunday for me. It was kind of you."

The solicitor smiled. "You're very welcome, Jake. I wouldn't have done it for anybody, of course, but I had much respect for Mr Walker."

Jake turned and headed off towards the park. He looked at his watch and realised that he had been in the solicitor's office for more than half an hour. All that time, just to read two pages of a letter! It was still drizzling, but it was more refreshing than annoying. Walking home through the park would help clear his mind, he thought. His family would certainly expect him to tell them what the letter said, so he'd have to concoct something pretty convincing. He carried on walking, deep in thought.

By the time he arrived home, his mother was just putting the finishing touches to one of her excellent roast lunches. The smell was delicious, and Jake was starving. His father came into the kitchen.

"Ah, the landlord has returned," he quipped. "Hey, in less than five years' time, your mother and I can come to your house for lunch!"

"Yeah, funny, Dad," said Jake with a smile.

"So?" asked his father.

"So what?"

"So what? So what did the letter say? Why the secrecy about reading it in the solicitor's office and then destroying it? Come on, spill the beans, son."

Jake had decided on his walk home that it would be better to stick, as far as possible, to the truth, although of course he couldn't mention the

Timekeepers. Neither did he want to mention anything about his true lineage.

"Well basically he wanted to explain why he'd left me the house. He said that he didn't have any relatives, and he didn't want to leave it to any charity or to the State. He said that I was about the closest thing he had to family, and that he knew we'd look after the house and garden properly."

"We?" echoed his father. "I hate gardening at the best of times in my own garden! What chance do we have of keeping his garden in the pristine condition that he kept it in? Maybe you'd better go to horticultural college rather than university."

"Oh, it's not that bad," said Jake's mother, coming to his defence. "The garden's really well established, so keeping it tidy shouldn't be too difficult. Ours, on the other hand, is an overgrown jungle which needs a lot of work. We're going to have to tackle it in the Spring."

His father decided to ignore that thought, and turned back to Jake.

"So why didn't he leave the house to Alice as well? I mean, your mother and I have got a house, and now you've got a house too. What about Alice?"

"Yeah, good point," said Alice. "You were obviously much closer to Mr Walker than I was, but what about me?"

"I don't know," said Jake. "It's not as if I could have a conversation with him about his reasons. It's what he wrote in the letter. But I'd thought about that too. I'll live there when I've finished university and, when you've finished, you can live there too. It'd be cool – just think, nobody telling you to tidy your room, or to turn your music down."

Alice thought about it for a second. "Yes, I like the sound of that."

"God, it'll be a complete pit. And a noisy one at that," said his father.

"Then later on we can either rent it out or sell it and split the proceeds," said Jake.

"Split the proceeds?" Alice looked almost speechless. "You mean half and half?"

"I don't see why not," said Jake. "It wouldn't seem fair for me to sell it and keep all the money."

"You'd be better off renting it out," said his father. "It's an investment, and it'll never lose money. But that's all for the future. So tell me, why did you have to destroy the letter? What was in it that he didn't want anybody else to see?"

Jake recounted the story he had devised on the way home from the solicitors.

"He said that he'd done something wrong when he was young. Nobody had ever found out about it, but he had always felt guilty."

"What, you mean he'd committed a crime?" asked Jake's mother.

"Yes," said Jake, "but nothing really serious. He hadn't committed a murder or anything like that. He'd met this guy in Africa who lived alone on a small farm. Mr Walker lived with him for a couple of years, helping out with the animals and the crops in return for food and accommodation, and painting in his spare time. Then this guy fell really sick and begged Mr Walker to take him back to England before he died. He had no relatives, and wanted to be buried beside his parents in the north of England somewhere. Mr Walker had been thinking about coming back anyway, so they travelled on the same ship together.

"Anyway, it was a long journey and the man didn't make it. He died shortly before they reached England. When Mr Walker went through his belongings, he found something like ten thousand pounds in cash – I guess that was a lot of money in those days. Since there were no relatives, Mr Walker decided to keep all of the money himself, but he still kept his promise and made sure the man had a decent burial in the same graveyard as his parents."

"Doesn't sound like a huge crime to me," said his father. "I'd have been tempted to do the same thing." Jake's mother shot him a glance. "What? It didn't belong to anybody else, did it? And the man it belonged to had died, so it's hardly stealing."

"Maybe," said his mother, "but it still wasn't his money."

"Yes, that's what he felt so guilty about," said Jake. "He'd come back to England almost penniless, and suddenly he had all this money which was just about enough to buy a house. It set him up for the rest of his life."

"So why tell you about it in a letter to be opened and destroyed after his death?" asked his father.

"He explained that too. He said he'd never been religious, but he didn't want to die with that on his conscience. I suppose he would have been too embarrassed to tell us in person, in case we stopped seeing him. So the letter was a kind of confession, and he wanted it to be destroyed so that it wouldn't go any further."

"Well, it's all ancient history as far as I can see," said his father. "Nobody else had a claim on that money. Strange, though. I remember him telling me that his mother had left him the money for his house."

"That was obviously his cover story," said Jake's mother, with a *sometimes-you-are-so-naïve* look on her face. "But I agree, I don't think it really matters now, not after all these years. It doesn't make me think any worse of him, anyway. He was still basically a good and decent man. If that's the worst thing he ever did, then so what?"

His father nodded. "My thoughts exactly. Right, what's for dessert, dear?"

Jake breathed a sigh of relief. It had been a rather elaborate tale, but it had had to be. He didn't think Mr Walker would have minded Jake's portrayal of him as a petty criminal on one occasion during his youth. After all, it was better than spilling any information about either his mother or the Timekeepers. His parents had believed it, and hadn't been too shocked. It had all happened so long ago anyway. No, thought Jake, it was unlikely they'd say any more about it, and they certainly wouldn't tell anyone else.

CHAPTER SEVENTEEN

Thinking about it a few weeks later, in the run up to Christmas, Jake realised how his life had changed completely from what it had been in June before his exams. School life was pretty much the same as usual, but Jake felt more like an adult and less like a child. He had responsibilities, including a house, and had done things which nobody would have believed.

"Hey, Jake!"

Jake stopped in his tracks, realising at the same instant that everything else had done so as well. Traveller was standing just behind him. Jake had been trudging to school, ignoring the cold wind which flew down the High Street.

"Hey, Traveller," he said. "I haven't seen you for a while. What's up?"

"Need your help again, I'm afraid. Can you find somewhere to disappear?"

"What's wrong with here?"

"It's a daylight job – real time, not the future. We don't want people to see you disappear from the High Street whenever you stop time."

Jake looked around. "There's a public toilet just over there at the entrance to the park," he said.

"Okay. Once I've gone, get in there quickly and wait for me to come and get you."

"Alright. What's the job, though?"

"There's an armed bank robbery going on in London. I'll bring Splitter with me, and he can get us there."

"Will it be dangerous?" asked Jake.

"Shouldn't be. Nothing's dangerous when you can stop time, is it? Now, back in position please." Jake did as he was told.

The Traveller vanished. As soon as he'd gone, Jake sprinted across the road to the entrance of the park, and into the toilet. It was horrible. Stainless steel everywhere, much of it covered in graffiti, and a strong smell of disinfectant. Within seconds, he was joined by the Traveller and Splitter.

"Hmm, nice place you've got here, Jake," said Splitter with a grin, glancing around and screwing up his face in mock disgust.

"Funny one, Splitter," said Jake. "There aren't exactly many hiding places in the High Street."

"We'd better get going," said Traveller.

"Who found out about the robbery anyway?" asked Jake.

"Splitter did," said Traveller. "It's one of his hobbies, scanning police radio transmissions – he's a bit nerdy like that."

"Charming description," said Splitter. "Actually, Freezer, it's quite informative. There's always something interesting happening, and quite often I can help them out – without them knowing it, of course."

"Well, let's see what we can do this time," said Traveller. "Jake, don't forget to stop time as soon as we arrive." Jake nodded. "Okay, ready?"

They linked arms, and Splitter clicked his fingers. Instantly, they found themselves in a small deserted alleyway.

Click!

They detached themselves and looked around.

"The bank's just round the corner up there," said Splitter, pointing to the end of the alley.

They moved forward together, safe in the knowledge that they needed neither to hurry or avoid being seen. When they reached the end of the alley, they turned the corner and to see a static scene which could have been drawn from a Hollywood movie. Police cars and vans filled the street, which had been cordoned off at both ends. Several policemen were dressed in helmets and flak jackets, with firearms pointing at the doors of the bank.

"There's been a stand-off for about half an hour now," said Splitter. "According to the radio broadcasts I picked up, the police reckon there are four armed robbers inside. They've got hostages, and have threatened to start shooting if the police prevent them from leaving."

"Let's go and have a look inside before we decide what to do," said Traveller.

They slipped under the police cordon and threaded their way through the armed police to the doors of the bank. Traveller went in first, followed by Splitter and Jake. Inside, they saw about a dozen customers all lying face down on the floor, their hands clasped behind their heads. Most had their eyes closed. Despite the static scene, a smell of fear and tension filled the air.

The four armed robbers, their appearance made more menacing by the black balaclavas which covered their faces, were standing together in a corner behind the entrance. Two of them had a large black sports bag

117

in one hand, and a handgun in the other. The others held what looked like short barrelled shotguns. The robber nearest the door – the ringleader, Jake guessed – stood behind a hostage, his arm wrapped around the woman's chest.

"Looks as though they're just about to move outside," said Traveller. "Things could get nasty. Let's get back to a safe place and let things run for a couple of minutes to see what happens."

"Can't we do anything else in here first?" asked Jake.

"No, best not," said Traveller. "We don't want the robbers to notice anything unusual at this stage, otherwise they might start hurting the hostages. The time to act is when they're outside. Let's just hope they don't run out shooting."

The three of them left the bank and returned to the corner of the alleyway. Once safely out of sight of the police, Traveller turned to Jake.

"Alright, let things run and we'll see what happens. If nothing happens after a couple of minutes, we might have to come up with some other idea to help the situation along."

Click!

The radio on the lapel of the nearest policeman crackled into life.

"Hold your positions. It looks like they might be coming out. Nobody is to fire unless ordered to. All teams in position and ready? Confirm, please." "Team one in position and ready." "Team two in position and ready." "Team three in position and ready." "Okay, standby for further orders…"

There was a moment of silence, and then:

"They're coming out. There's a hostage. Hold your fire, hold your fire!"

Traveller risked a quick glance around the corner. All eyes were fixed on the robbers and their hostage, so he was not seen. All four robbers now stood just outside the bank, with the lead robber holding the hostage tight in front of him. The other three brandished their guns at the police menacingly.

The lead robber shouted, "Clear the way! No shooting, or the lady dies!"

"This is it," whispered Traveller. "Jake, when you're ready?"

Click!

"Great. Let's see what we can do."

Traveller, Splitter and Jake headed for the bank, taking in the situation around them as they went. One or two of the armed policemen looked nervous, while the others just looked frightening. All guns were aimed at the robbers, who were seriously outnumbered. But they had a hostage and, for the moment at least, that gave them an advantage.

"Anyone got any ideas?" asked Splitter when they reached the group of robbers.

"Um, I do," said Jake.

The others looked at him.

"Okay, shoot – I mean, go ahead," said Traveller.

"As I see it," said Jake, "there are two ways in which we can help. We can retrieve all the money, and we can try to make sure that the hostages don't get hurt."

"Excellent," said Traveller. "What do you recommend we do?"

"We need to find something as a substitute for the money. Maybe something like paper shreddings, but we'd need lots of it."

"There must be some inside the bank. I'll go and have a look. But I reckon we'll need a bit more weight – paper shreds are very light, much lighter than wads of notes."

Jake looked up and down the road. "There's a fruit stall up there, just inside the police cordon. Nobody seems to be watching it."

"A fruit stall?" echoed Splitter. "Here we are, right in the middle of a potentially lethal situation, and you're talking about fruit? Didn't you have any breakfast this morning?"

Jake rolled his eyes at Traveller, who nodded in agreement. "Not fruit to eat, stupid! We add some fruit or vegetables to the bags, to give them more weight."

"Oh, I see. Er – what are we going to do with the money?"

"Put it back inside the bank, I suppose," said Jake. "That's where it belongs."

"I know, but I don't suppose – "

"Don't even go there, Splitter," said Traveller.

"What?"

"No, you can't have any. It goes back into the bank."

"Spoilsport," said Splitter.

"Jake, get the bags. Be very careful, though. There are a couple of TV cameras just over there, as well as a police helicopter up there. They're bound to be focussing on the gang quite closely, so we don't want them to notice anything unusual."

As gently as he could, Jake lifted the bags from each of the two robbers. They were quite heavy. He put them on the ground and unzipped them. They were stuffed full of money, bundles and bundles of notes.

Splitter whistled softly. "Wow, there must be half a million pounds there, if not more."

"Do they weigh about the same?" asked Traveller.

Jake weighed both bags together. "Yeah, I guess so."

"Okay, I'll check inside for some paper shreddings, or anything else we can put in. You go and get some fruit and vegetables from the stall up the road. I'd say potatoes and oranges are best – they're about the right weight compared to a bundle of notes."

"Take my hand, Jake," said Splitter. "I'll split there, and we can bring a box of stuff back, it'll be quicker and easier than walking."

Jake took hold of his hand. Splitter clicked, and they were suddenly standing by the fruit stall. Jake looked back.

"Hey, is that still you, standing outside the bank?" he asked.

"Yes," said Splitter. "That means I'm now in three places at once. Come on, let's get a move on. I start feeling dizzy if I stay in three places for too long – too much to concentrate on."

They put a selection of fruit and vegetables in a cardboard box. They wouldn't need too many, Jake guessed, so it was unlikely that the stall owner would notice anything missing. He picked up the box and tucked it under one arm. Then they linked up again and Splitter clicked, taking them back to the front of the bank.

A few moments later, Traveller came out through the front door, carrying a large plastic sack of shredded paper.

"I found three shredding machines," he said. "Banks shred everything, so there's always plenty of shredded paper around."

"Okay, let's do one bag at a time," said Jake. "That way we'll know if the weight is about right. Put some of the shredded paper in first, and we'll add the heavier stuff if we need to. If we put the food in first, the bag might look lumpy."

They emptied the money from the first sports bag, and Traveller carefully transferred handfuls of shredded paper. Jake added a few potatoes and oranges, and weighed the bags again.

"Too light," he said. "It's the right size, but you can tell it's much lighter."

They took out some of the shredded paper and added a few more oranges. Jake zipped it up and weighed them again.

"Perfect," he said. "Here, you two try it, see what you think." Splitter and Traveller both weighed the bags. They agreed that the weight and size was about right. They emptied the second bag and filled it with the same combination of shredded paper, potatoes and oranges. When they were satisfied that both bags looked and weighed the same as they had before, Splitter took the box back to the fruit stall. Traveller took the rest of the paper shreddings inside the bank, while Jake carefully put the bags back into the hands of the two robbers. It was unlikely, in the heat of the moment, that a slight difference in weight would be noticed.

The three of them picked up all the bundles of notes between them and carried them into the bank. They found the vault, still open, and put the money on the empty shelves.

"Well, that's the money taken care of," said Traveller as they went back outside. "What about the hostages, Jake?"

"This lady is the one in most danger," said Jake, "but the others might still be at risk if the robbers decide to go back into the bank. I say we should check the guns, and remove all the bullets."

"Brilliant," said Traveller. "Just what I'd have done."

One by one, they took the guns from the robbers. They were all fully loaded. Jake was horrified: these guys obviously weren't amateurs. Traveller emptied the magazines from the handguns, and checked that the chambers were empty. He put the bullets in his pocket. He broke open the shotguns and took the two cartridges out of each of them. They put the guns back into the correct hands, and stepped back to survey the scene.

"Looks about right," said Traveller. "Anything else we can do?"

"How about removing the balaclavas?" suggested Jake.

"Hmm, bit unnecessary, really," said Traveller. "They haven't got any bullets and, even if they did manage to escape, they've only got some shredded paper for their efforts."

"Okay, how about tying their shoelaces together?"

"Do what?"

"It's something I wanted to do at school once – someone who was giving me a hard time. It'd be perfect for this. They're unarmed, and the police would catch them straight away."

"Hey, I like it," said Splitter. "It won't be as visible as removing their balaclavas, but it'd create just as much confusion."

"Yeah, I like it too," said Traveller. "Let's do it."

The gang of robbers were all wearing trainers. Tying the laces together was easy, and only took a couple of minutes.

"Right, let's get back to the alleyway," said Traveller. "I'd like to see what happens."

They walked back to the alley and turned the corner.

"Shall I let it roll?" asked Jake.

"Sure, why not?" said Traveller. "Should be fun to watch. But we can't hang around for long – just long enough to make sure the gang gets caught."

Click!

A policeman with a megaphone stood up behind one of the police cars.

"Release the hostage and drop your weapons. You are completely surrounded. There is no way out."

"I'm telling you, I'll kill her," shouted the lead robber. The lady started sobbing silently, holding onto the robber's forearm around her chest.

"Release the hostage, and you will not be harmed."

"I'll count to three," shouted the robber. "Clear the way or she gets it!"

The police remained in their positions.

"One....two....Don't make me do it!....Three!"

The woman screamed. Even from where they were standing, they could hear the empty click of the shotgun which was pointed at the woman's ribcage. The robber looked down at his gun, shook it, and pulled the trigger again. Click. Jake and the others were horrified: the robber would actually have shot his hostage.

The confusion began. One of the other robbers aimed his gun in the air and pulled the trigger. Again, nothing happened. Twice more he pulled the trigger. Click, click. The lead robber glanced at his colleagues, then roughly pushed the woman away in front of him and turned to run. Almost instantly, he tumbled to the ground, dropping his gun as he tried to break his fall. As he did so, his colleagues instinctively started to bolt in all different directions, with the same results. It was almost comical to watch.

Within seconds, the police pounced on the gang. Several armed officers rushed forward, guns aimed at the robbers, all shouting "Stay down!" or "Don't move!". The robbers put up no resistance, and stretched their arms out in front of them.

Once the robbers had been securely handcuffed, their balaclavas were removed. They all looked shocked and confused. One policeman picked up the sports bag and opened it. He stared at the contents for a second, then picked up a handful of shredded paper and held it above the bag. He let the shreds fall between his fingers, into the bag or onto the pavement. Then he picked an orange out of the bag, and held it up to show his colleagues. He delved further, but there was no money to be found. He did the same with the other bag. Three of the robbers looked on in utter astonishment, while the ringleader simply kept his head down.

The policemen hauled the robbers to their feet and started walking towards a van. But all of the robbers fell over again at the first step. Two policemen also stumbled as they tried to keep their prisoners upright. Closer inspection revealed the tied shoelaces, causing further perplexion among both the robbers and their captors.

"We've seen enough," said Traveller, smiling broadly. "Brilliant job, Jake."

"Thanks," said Jake, still replaying the final scene over and over in his mind.

"Come on, we'd better get back or we'll be spotted. Splitter?"

"Okay, I'm ready. Boy, what a blast that was!"

They linked arms, Splitter clicked and they were instantly back in the public convenience in the park.

Traveller patted Jake's arm. "I'll look forward to seeing that particular story on the news tonight," he said. "Thanks again for your help, Jake." He looked at his watch. "Sorry, it looks like I might have made you a little late for school."

"That's okay," he said. "It's only up the road and I can be there in a couple of minutes. There's just enough time." He hesitated. "You know, if we hadn't been there today, that poor woman would actually have been shot. It would have been on live television as well."

"Yes," said Traveller. "In our line of work, we can sometimes come across the most evil people in the world. That makes it all the more rewarding when we help them get caught, I suppose. But, hey, we saved a life today, Jake. That makes me feel good."

"Yeah, me too. I guess it was lucky that Splitter was listening to the police radio."

"True. Come on, Splitter, time to go."

"Cheers, Jake," said Splitter.

"See you around."

Traveller and Splitter linked arms, Splitter clicked his fingers and they disappeared.

Jake picked up his school bag and left..

CHAPTER EIGHTEEN

Jake was on his way home later that afternoon when Fergus caught up with him in the High Street.

"Jake, let's talk."

"Sorry, Fergus, not today. I'm knackered."

"After this morning's activities, perhaps?" said Fergus.

Jake stopped dead in his tracks and turned to him. "What?"

Fergus took him lightly by the arm. There was a hint of aggression in his grip, although he was still smiling amicably. "Cup of tea, I think," he said, steering him towards The Chill Zone. "We've got a lot to talk about."

Jake sighed, and resigned himself to another of Fergus' grillings. He went to the furthest corner of the café and dropped his bag on the sofa sulkily before sitting down next to it. He waited for Fergus to come over with the tea. Today there were cakes too. What was Fergus up to, thought Jake. Still, free tea and cake was rarely something that Jake wanted to decline, even from Fergus.

"So," said Fergus as he spread the contents of the tray on the table between them. He sat down in one of the armchairs opposite Jake. "How are you?"

"Look, this is very nice of you, but I don't have too much time today," said Jake.

"Oh, that's alright. I'm sure you'll find time for this."

"And what's that supposed to mean?"

Fergus looked triumphant.

"I saw you," he said. "Or, to put it another way, I've got the evidence I needed."

"What are you on about?" asked Jake, feeling less comfortable as the conversation went on.

"Don't worry, it's not any evidence that I can use, but it proves I'm right. I'm right! You *are* a Timekeeper!"

Jake tried to keep his face impassive. "We've had that conversation."

"Yes, but not since this morning."

"This morning?"

It was Fergus' turn to sigh. "This morning. Come on, Jake, do I really have to spell it out for you?"

"Apparently, yes," said Jake. "What are you on about?"

Fergus leaned forward in his chair, clasping his fingers together.

"I was sitting in here this morning, over by the window, when you passed by. I presume you were on your way to school. You stopped for a second, then dashed across the road to the toilets in the park."

"Stomach trouble," said Jake. "I got caught short, so what?"

"Yes, that's what I presumed, at first. But out of pure curiosity, I followed you."

"You what?"

"Yes, and guess what I saw when I went into the toilets?"

"What did you see?"

"That's just it. I saw nothing. Oh, your school bag was in the cubicle, but you weren't. In fact, you weren't in the toilets at all. I saw you go in, there's only one entrance, and then you...disappear."

"People don't disappear, Fergus. Of course I was in there."

"No, no, you weren't. There was just your school bag. So where were you?"

Jake said nothing. It was clear that Fergus had another vital piece of the puzzle, but there were still pieces missing.

"Then I saw the news. That bank robbery which went wrong. It was all on live television – bags with no money in them, all four robbers falling over as soon as they tried to run away – it was quite farcical. To anybody else, they simply looked inept, but not to me. I think you were there, somehow, causing them to be caught."

"That's ridiculous," said Jake. "The robbery took place in the middle of London. How on earth could I have had anything to do with them being caught?"

"I don't know that – yet," said Fergus. "But you certainly weren't in the toilet a couple of minutes after you went in. But that's not all."

"No?"

"I waited a few minutes outside. Then I heard some voices from within. Two, or maybe three. I couldn't make out what they were saying, but there were definitely people inside the toilet. Then you come out on your own, and start running off to school. I went inside and – guess what? – there was nobody there. Now you can't tell me I was imagining it. I wasn't. I was there. I saw it, and I heard it. You were there, then you weren't. Then there were two or three people, then only you, and then nobody. But you were the only person who went in and came out of the entrance to the toilet – apart from me, of course.

Sounds confusing? It is. So please, drop the pretence and enlighten me."

"I'm sorry, I can't."

"Look, I've already said that I don't have any evidence. I didn't have a video camera with me – more's the pity. But you can't deny it any longer. You are a Timekeeper – and you're not alone, I presume, judging by the other voices I heard. You have the power, somehow, to disappear and reappear, stopping time without anybody else noticing."

Jake said nothing. He felt completely cornered. There was no way he could tell Fergus anything, but further denials seemed pointless. He needed some advice.

Click!

He took out the pocket watch and turned half the minute hand to the number ten before releasing the crown. All the Timekeepers appeared at once.

"Jake," said Traveller. "So soon after this morn – " he noticed Fergus sitting there.

"Sorry to get you all here," said Jake, "but I think this is an emergency, and I need your advice."

They sat down wherever they could – on the arms of the sofa, the arm of Jake's chair, the two free chairs around Jake's coffee table.

"What's going on?" asked Traveller.

"Fergus followed me this morning," said Jake. "He was sitting in here this morning, over by the window, when I passed by on my way to school. He saw me dash across to the toilets in the park, and he followed me. When he went in, I wasn't there. It must have been during the time we let things run at the bank. He waited outside the toilets, and said he heard two or three voices – though he didn't hear what was said – before I came out alone. After I had gone, he checked again, but there was nobody else inside. He challenged me about it, said it was the evidence he'd been looking for to prove that I was a Timekeeper, although he knew he still had no evidence that he could publish."

"How did you react?" asked Traveller.

"I tried to deny it, of course, but it was pretty pointless. He knew what he'd seen. That's when I called you. I don't know how to handle it. But…"

"But what?"

127

"Well, I think there are three options," said Jake. "You might have other ideas, but I've been giving it some thought ever since Fergus first latched onto me."

"Go on," said Traveller. Although there was no prospect of being overheard, the others leaned in closer to listen.

"First, we could tell Fergus that he's right. Of course, we couldn't tell him everything. It would have to be the absolute minimum to confirm what he knows. Second, you and Retro could take him back in time again. We find the note he left himself, and destroy it. Lastly, I just continue to deny it."

"And which option do you favour?"

"It's really hard. There are advantages and disadvantages with each. If I tell him that he's right, I could make it a condition that he never publishes another word about us. Seeker can check to see if he keeps his word. If we take him back in time, we might not be able to find the note, and we'd be back where we started. We don't know where the note is, even now. If I continue to deny it, he'll just carry on challenging me. He still won't have any proof, which means people still won't believe him, but I might have to take out a restraining order against him just like Mr Walker did. Personally, I think the best option would be to tell him some of the truth. The poor guy's almost gone crazy trying to prove it, and everybody else thinks he really is crazy already. He doesn't know why he wrote the note he found, and it's already ruined his career. It just doesn't seem fair."

"I agree," said Retro, "but he did bring it upon himself, didn't he? I mean, he messed up being a Timekeeper, which is why he left himself the note as insurance. I never worked with him and I've never even met the bloke, but I don't have too much sympathy."

Traveller shook his head. "I know what you're saying, but telling him the truth could be a huge mistake. He's a journalist, remember? He's spent half his life chasing this story just so that he can print it. I'm not sure he'd stick to any guarantee he gave us. And we'd have to spend so much time checking up on him. Then again, I don't think it's worth us taking him back in time again either. As you said, there's no guarantee we could find the note. He may have left himself some other piece of insurance too. No, I think our only option is to carry on denying it. The secret is just too great, and it goes against all our principles to reveal it to anybody, for whatever reason."

"I guess you're right," said Jake.

"I might be, and I might not be. I am aware, though, that it's you who has to face Fergus. It'll be tough on you, I know, and I'm sorry about that." He looked around the group. "Are we all agreed?"

They each nodded. Protection of the secret was paramount to all of them, and it was just too risky to reveal it to Fergus.

"Okay," said Jake.

"You might just have to get tough with Fergus, Jake," said Traveller. "I know he won't give up, so it might be best to tell him that you're just going to ignore him from now on if he carries on. And remind him that you'll call the police if he causes any trouble or follows you around."

"Yes," said Jake, "although I hope it doesn't come to that. I like him, in a way, and I feel sorry for him."

"Me too," said Traveller. "I think we all do, but we've got to put the Timekeepers before our personal feelings about the man. He'll survive, even if people think he's mad."

"Thanks for the advice," said Jake, looking around the group. "I'd probably have done the wrong thing."

"It's a tough one," said Seeker. "You did the right thing in getting us all together."

"Yes," agreed Retro. "If you need to talk about it any time, we're here for you, Jake."

"I appreciate that – sorry, I don't even know your real names. It seems a bit odd to keep calling you by your titles when we have an informal meeting."

"Good point," said Traveller. "I'm Martin."

"Suzy," said Retro.

"Annie," said Seeker.

"Kevin," said Splitter.

"Well, thanks everyone," said Jake.

"Come on, guys, let's go," said Traveller to the rest of the group. "Good luck, Jake."

"I think I'm going to need it."

Jake took out his pocket watch and reunited the two halves of the minute hand. He let go of the crown, and his colleagues disappeared at once. He got back into position and took a deep breath.

Click!

"As I said, I'm sorry, Fergus. I can't help you."

"Can't? Or won't?"

"It doesn't really matter, does it? Let it go – please."

Fergus stared at him for a moment. He looked crestfallen, deflated. He'd come so close to learning at least a part of the truth and now, once again, he'd come up against a brick wall. It was almost like being back at square one, despite having seen evidence of the Timekeepers with his own eyes. Jake stared back defiantly. It was hard, but Jake knew that Fergus would exploit any hint of weakness.

Fergus shrugged his shoulders. "You know I can't," he said quietly. "Not now. I've got to find out, somehow."

"Look – I don't think I can see you again," said Jake.

"Why not?"

"It's just – "

Realisation crept over Fergus' face, and his eyes opened wide.

"You've just met your friends again, haven't you? The ones you were speaking to in the toilets in the park. Were they here? Are they still here?" He looked around wildly.

"No – "

"Or did you go and see them? You stopped time again, right here in front of me."

"No – "

"They told you not to talk to me any more, didn't they? They've put the screws on you. I'm getting too close, aren't I? They've – "

Jake stood up. "That's enough, Fergus. Enough." Fergus' eyes were dancing in his head as he tried to figure out some rational explanation. "Nobody was here, and I haven't moved from this seat. Stopped time in front of you? Jesus, what an imagination! You need to get help."

"So help me, Jake." There was a pleading look on his face. "Won't you?"

"It's not my help you need, Fergus. You need to see a professional. Maybe they will be able to convince you that you've got to let this go. Nobody believes what you say about the Timekeepers."

"But I'm right, dammit. If you won't help me, then I'll have to find another way to prove it." There was a fierce determination in his eyes.

"Like what?" asked Jake.

"I don't know yet. But I do know that I don't need to see a shrink. You know that too."

"I hope you're not going to follow me again," said Jake. "I still mean it when I say I'll call the police."

Fergus smiled. "No, I don't need to follow you around any more. I followed you today, remember, and I got the proof I was looking for.

130

For the first time, I witnessed something that I'd only ever had second-hand reports of before. I'm getting closer, Jake. After all the years of being discredited, after all the humiliation I've had to endure, I'm not going to give up now. I'll find a way to prove it, clear my name. I'll – "

"God, Fergus, just give it up!" said Jake firmly. "You're talking like a maniac. This thing has taken over your life. It's an obsession. You'll kill yourself if you carry on like this."

Fergus stopped in his tracks and looked at Jake. "Kill myself?"

"You know what I mean," said Jake quietly.

Fergus was staring off into the distance, as if deep in thought. There was an empty pause.

"Fergus?" prompted Jake, bringing Fergus out of his short reverie.

"What? Oh, yes," said Fergus. His eyes suddenly lit up, and he smiled. "You know, Jake, you're right. You're absolutely right!" There was a strangely triumphant look on his face.

"I am?" asked Jake, astonished.

"Yes, yes, you're right." Fergus jumped up and took Jake's hand, shaking it vigorously. "Thanks," he said.

Now it was Jake's turn to be confused. "For what?"

"Er – for…the chat. Thanks." He was still pumping Jake's hand.

Jake was worried now. He pulled his hand free. "Are you alright, Fergus?"

"Alright? Yes, of course I'm alright. I'm fine. Never felt better. Now, if you'll excuse me, I have to be getting along. Things to do, and all that."

"Sure," said Jake. He watched as Fergus slurped down the rest of his tea, picked up his bag and walked quickly out of the café without even a backwards glance.

Jake picked up his school bag and left the café. He played the scene over and over in his mind as he walked slowly home through the park, but he simply couldn't figure it out. Why had Fergus changed so suddenly? One minute he was depressed and angry, and the next he was cheerful, almost ecstatic. Of course he'd been right about Jake being a Timekeeper, and he would have known that Jake was holding back some vital information. He'd even been right that Jake had stopped time in front of him, although that had presumably just been a wild guess. For a journalist, all that should have made Fergus even more determined to sit there and drag out any confirmation that he could get from Jake, but he had suddenly bolted. It was bizarre behaviour, but then Fergus was rather a bizarre person.

As he arrived home, Jake decided that there was no point in trying to work it out. He would have to wait and see what Fergus did next. He was sure Fergus had some wacky idea up his sleeve, and it was only a matter of time before Jake would find out what it was. A triple decker peanut butter sandwich took his mind off it, and he went upstairs to play a computer game.

CHAPTER NINETEEN

It was snowing. The school term had finished, and Christmas was only a few days away. As usual, the houses in Duckworth Close appeared to hold an unofficial competition to see who could deck their house in the brightest, most colourful lights. Only Mr Walker's house had remained in darkness, until the other night when Jake had bought an extra set of lights and spent an afternoon hanging them around the front windows. Some other residents had chipped in, out of respect, and the entire street once again looked so festive that it became a local tourist attraction. There was a two-page spread in the local paper with photographs of various houses and, some nights, there was a constant stream of traffic in the Close as local residents came to have a look at the lights.

The shops were full of people doing their last minute Christmas shopping. Women were queuing in the butchers for fresh turkey, and all the shops in the High Street were doing a roaring trade.

Jake and Alice were shopping together, trying to decide what Christmas presents to buy for their parents. It was something they enjoyed doing each year, feeding off each other's excitement and looking for the most unusual gifts.

They were browsing through a department store when Alice suddenly nudged Jake.

"Hey, look over there. Did you see that?"

"See what?"

"That woman. She just put a jumper into her bag. She must be stealing it."

"Really?"

"Yeah. Just watch her – see if she takes anything else."

They watched the young woman, trying not to make it look obvious. The woman picked up a scarf with a matching pair of gloves and pretended to examine them closely. As she refolded the scarf, Jake and Alice saw the gloves fall into her open bag. It was well done. If they hadn't been watching her closely, they would have missed it. The woman appeared to rummage around in her bag, and then dropped something on the floor underneath a rack of clothes. When she had moved on, Alice rushed over and picked it up. It was the price tag.

She showed it to Jake. "Shouldn't we tell somebody?"

"Let's wait and see if she takes anything else."

"But she's already stolen at least two things, and she's removed the labels. If she walks through the detectors, the alarm won't sound. She'll get clean away with it."

"I don't think she'll succeed."

"Why not?"

"Er – let's just see. Look, she's heading for the door now."

Click!

Everything came to a halt. The woman froze, a few feet from the door towards which she had been striding confidently. Jake looked around, and picked a few items off a nearby costume jewellery stall. They all had labels on. He slipped them into the woman's bag, and returned to his position next to Alice.

Click!

The woman strode on. As she passed between the detectors, a shrill alarm sounded. She looked around quickly, and decided to make a run for it. Two guards were on her almost at once. They each held an arm, and one of them opened the woman's bag. He picked out the gloves and a jumper. The woman could be heard protesting loudly that they were hers, that she'd bought them with her in case it got cold. Then the guard picked out one, two, three pairs of earrings and a bracelet, all with electronic security tags on. The woman was amazed.

"I didn't put them in there," she shouted. "I've never seen them before in my life."

"Let's go back inside, shall we, madam?" said one of the guards, who clearly tightened his grip on her arm. "We can sort it all out there."

"No," shouted the woman. "Somebody put them in my bag, I tell you."

"Did they really?" asked the guard. "Come on, love, back inside please. You can tell that to the security manager. We can't have people putting jewellery in innocent lady's handbags now, can we?"

The woman looked miserable as she realised that they were not going to let her go. She trudged back into the store, trying to shake off the iron grip of her two captors.

"Well," said Alice. "At least they caught her. It was a bit dumb of her to remove the tags from the clothes but not from the jewellery, wasn't it?"

"Yes," said Jake. "Looks like she might not have such a happy Christmas after all."

They continued browsing for a while, until Alice said,

"Let's split up for a while. I need to get a present for you, and you've got to spend some of your new fortune on me."

"What fortune?" said Jake. "It's not mine until I'm 21, and even then it's all bricks and mortar rather than cash."

"Well, at least you've got it coming to you, so you can afford to be a bit more generous this year, can't you? I've seen a really cool music system with surround sound..."

"Yeah, in your dreams. Okay, let's meet up again in an hour – in The Coffee Pot?"

"Alright. That should be enough time. It shouldn't take me long to find a huge wallet."

"Make sure it's a full one, then."

Once Alice was out of sight, Jake slipped back into the department store and picked up a few things that he knew she would like. A new CD from her favourite pop band, a bottle of perfume and a selection of hair stuff – Alice spent hours doing her hair in different styles: it never looked the same from one day to the next.

He was in The Coffee Pot in good time, and settled down with a mug of hot chocolate to wait. He immersed himself in his book of Sudoku puzzles – the new craze of increasingly difficult number crosswords that was sweeping school, and apparently the nation.

Alice turned up after half an hour, loaded down with shopping bags.

"Blimey," said Jake, "you've been busy."

"Yes, well I found what I wanted for you quite quickly, and then I found lots and lots of things that I wanted for me, so I thought I'd better buy them."

"Typical," said Jake. "I thought all those things were for me."

"Just the smallest one," she replied.

"Just as long as it's not the cheapest too. Otherwise I'll have to take yours back and – "

He was interrupted by the sound of his mobile phone ringing. He pulled it out of his pocket and looked at the screen.

Number withheld, it flashed. He answered it.

"Jake, it's me." The voice sounded vaguely familiar.

"Who?"

"Fergus."

"Oh." Jake's heart sank. He could do without Fergus hassling him again. "What do you want now?"

"I want you to come and meet me." It sounded more like a demand than a request.

"What, now?"

"Yes, now."

"Sorry, I'm busy." He was fed up with Fergus demanding meetings whenever it took his fancy. "Maybe tomorrow, if I feel like it."

"I may not be here tomorrow," said Fergus.

"Why – are you going away somewhere?" At least Christmas would be more pleasant if you did, thought Jake.

"Come to the window of the café," said Fergus.

"What?" said Jake, getting increasingly cross. "Are you watching me or something?"

"Just do it." Another instruction.

With an exaggerated sigh of boredom, Jake stood up. Alice looked up at him quizzically, and followed him as he walked over to the window. "What is this, a game or something?" he asked.

"Oh, no," said Fergus. "No game this time: I'm fed up with playing games. This time it's serious." There was a pause. "Ah, I can see you now."

"Where are you?" asked Jake, scanning the street in front of him.

"I'm not down there," said Fergus. "I'm up here. Look over to your left, and you'll see the multi storey car park. That's right, I'm up here – on the top."

Jake's eyes followed Fergus' directions, and he suddenly gasped. Fergus was standing on the wall of the very top level of the car park. Alice saw him too, and covered her mouth in alarm.

"Good," said Fergus. "It sounds like you've seen me."

"What are you doing up there?" asked Jake. "You could fall off."

"Yes, I could," said Fergus. "Or I could jump…"

"Jump? Why on earth would you do that?"

"Why not?" said Fergus. "Look at me. I'm a failure, and all because of the Timekeepers. My life's a mess, I've been discredited as a journalist, and nobody believes that I can write a serious story any more. Even though I'm right about the Timekeepers, nobody is prepared to listen. What's the point in going on?"

"It can't be that bad," said Jake.

"Can't it?" said Fergus. "What would you know about it? You're partly to blame for my situation – you and your chums, whoever they are." He paused to let the accusation sink in. "So it's come to this. I'm

136

giving you one last chance, Jake. Be up here in five minutes or I'll jump, and you'll have my death on your conscience for the rest of your life!"

The line went dead as Fergus hung up.

Jake saw him put the phone back in his pocket and stand upright, looking straight ahead of him instead of down at the café. Jake put his own phone away.

"What's he doing?" asked Alice.

"He said he wants me to go and talk to him. If I'm not there in five minutes, he said he'll jump."

"What?" She was horrified. "Why?"

Jake hesitated. "It's a long story," he said. He still hadn't taken his eyes off Fergus. "I'll have to go."

"But shouldn't we call the police or something?"

"No time for that," said Jake. "Besides, I don't think he's really serious."

"Yeah, but what if you're wrong?" said Alice. "Jake, this is crazy."

"I'd better go." He moved towards the door.

She blocked his way. "Then I'm coming with you," she said.

"No," he snapped.

She looked hurt. "Why not?"

He immediately felt guilty for being so sharp with her. "I'm sorry," he said. "Please, just stay here. I don't want you to be involved."

"Involved? In what?"

Jake looked at his watch. He didn't have time for this conversation right now. "Look, I'll explain when I get back, I promise. He said I had to be up there in five minutes."

He made a move to get past her, but she held her ground stubbornly. "No, Jake, I'm coming with you."

He opened his mouth to argue, but she put her hand up to stop him. "We stay together, right? I'm not letting you go up there alone. Who knows what he might do when you get to him?"

Jake realised he had no choice. "Alright," he said. "Let's go, but just leave the talking to me, okay?"

Alice smiled and nodded. She moved to one side, and followed him as he went past her and out of the café. They went as fast as they could, threading their way through the throng of shoppers. To Jake's huge relief, they all seemed oblivious to the fact that a man was standing on a ledge high above them, threatening to jump off.

Once in the car park, they ran up the stairs two at a time. He would have done that even if he hadn't been in a hurry, Jake realised as he looked around him. Graffiti was daubed on every available inch of wall space, and the floor was covered with litter. Then there was the smell – reminiscent of the toilets in the park – and, on the first level, there was even a puddle of vomit.

"Uurrr – how *gross!*" said Alice, holding her nose.

It was a relief when they reached the top level, pushing open the door and sucking the fresh, cold air into their lungs. Fergus was on the far side of the car park, and he turned to face them as they approached.

"Ah, Jake," he said with a smile. "I see you've brought your sister as well."

"We were shopping together, if you must know," said Jake.

"Yes, of course. And does she know about your little secret, too?" asked Fergus.

Alice looked from Fergus to Jake. "What little secret?" she asked.

Jake ignored her. "Leave Alice out of this. It's nothing to do with her, we were just out shopping together."

"So she doesn't know?" sneered Fergus. "Well, Jake, why don't you educate both of us at the same time?"

Alice tugged at Jake's sleeve. "What's he talking about?"

"I'm talking about your brother being a Timekeeper, Alice," said Fergus.

"Oh yeah, right," said Alice sarcastically.

Jake tried to change the subject. "You're not seriously going to jump, Fergus. Why don't you just get down from there and get on with your life?"

"Oh, I've never been more serious about anything," replied Fergus. "In fact, you gave me the idea."

"What idea?"

"The idea of killing myself."

"That's rubbish," said Jake. He suddenly realised what Fergus was talking about. "What, you mean when I said you'd kill yourself if you carried on about the Timekeepers? That was just a figure of speech! You know that as well as I do."

"A figure of speech, yes," said Fergus. "But it was also a brilliant idea."

"To kill yourself? Don't be stupid."

"No, Jake, I'm not being stupid. You see, it's a brilliant way of getting undeniable proof that the Timekeepers exist – and that you're one of them, of course."

Alice could keep quiet no longer. "Jake, what *is* he on about?"

Jake wished he'd left Alice in the café. It was staring to be awkward, having her listen to Fergus.

"Fergus thinks I'm a Timekeeper," he said, trying hard to make it sound like a ridiculous notion. "He thinks that there are several Timekeepers all running around doing brave things like saving people's lives. I keep telling him to give up the idea, but he just won't listen, and now he seems to blame me for his life being so sad. He says he'll keep on trying to prove it to the world." He turned back to Fergus. "So what now? What proof are you talking about this time?"

Fergus smiled, looking pleased with himself. "It's quite simple really. I jump off this car park."

"And you're pleased with that idea?" said Jake.

"It's a great idea!"

Jake and Alice exchanged glances. Alice shrugged her shoulders.

"Okay, so you're dead," said Jake, looking back at Fergus. "Then what?"

"That's just it, don't you see?" said Fergus. "That's why the plan is so simple, yet brilliant – even if I do say so myself."

"You've lost me, Fergus," said Jake. "I think you've finally cracked."

The smile vanished from Fergus' face, and was replaced by a look of pity.

"Oh dear, Jake. Sometimes you can be so dense. How on earth did they ever choose you to be a Timekeeper? Let me put it like this. If I'm right, I've got nothing to worry about. If I'm wrong, then I'll be dead and none of it will matter anyway. If you're not going to admit that you're a Timekeeper, we'll just have to put it to the ultimate test."

This is crazy, thought Jake. Would Fergus really throw himself off a high building just to test his theory? Is he just trying to get me to admit it, or would he really jump? He decided to find out.

"I'm not going to just stand here and watch you jump to your death," he said.

The smile returned. "Good, Jake. That's precisely what I'm counting on."

"No, Fergus." He took his phone out of his pocket. "I mean, I'm not having that on my conscience. You've got some wacky obsession about the Timekeepers, so if you want to jump, then jump, but don't try to make it my problem. I'm calling the police, and you can make it theirs instead."

"I wouldn't bother, Jake," said Fergus.

Jake stopped dialling and looked at him. "Why not?"

Fergus turned around and faced the abyss.

"Because they won't be here in time."

And he jumped.

CHAPTER TWENTY

Jake and Alice both reacted instinctively.

Alice grabbed Jake's arm in horror.

Click!

Alice ran towards the wall where Fergus had been standing. At first, Jake thought that he had not clicked his fingers. Then, with a sudden dread, he realised what had happened.

"Alice, wait!"

Too late. She had reached the wall. She looked over, screamed and staggered back with a hand covering her mouth. Jake brushed past her and looked down. There was Fergus, just a few feet below him, suspended in mid air. It was obviously the last thing Alice had expected to see, and she looked more shocked than if Fergus had been lying dead on the pavement so very far below.

"Alice."

She looked over the wall again, and then back at Jake.

"What's happening, Jake?" she asked.

Jake sighed. "It's true," he said quietly. "What Fergus said, it's true."

"You mean – ?"

"Yes, I am a Timekeeper."

Alice was in a state of panic. "Jake, Fergus is – he's just floating there, we've got to do something. What's going on? Why is he – how can he – "

Jake took her firmly by the shoulders. "Alice, listen to me!" The sudden sharpness in his voice stopped her in her tracks.

He was going to have to explain it all. He remembered how confusing it had been when Mr Walker had first explained it to him, and he knew it wouldn't be easy, especially in these circumstances. But in a way he also felt relieved. The secret would be safe with her, and he trusted her completely. First, he'd have to calm her down.

He leaned back against the wall. "Let me tell you what's happening now," he said, "and I can tell you the background later."

"But what about Fergus?" said Alice. "Shouldn't we – "

"Don't worry about him, he's quite safe – for the moment at least. Just listen to me, please."

Her anxiety subsided, and she waited for Jake to continue.

"Time has stopped," he said. "There's not much evidence of it up here, but have another look down in the High Street. Nothing's moving – people, cars, even Fergus. Listen to how quiet it is." She cocked her head, then nodded. She looked over the wall again and watched for any sign of movement, however small. She didn't see any. "You see? Everything's been frozen in time. Nothing will move again until I click my fingers."

She spun round and looked at him incredulously. "Until you *what*?"

"Click my fingers." She didn't look convinced. "I know it sounds weird, but it's true."

As Jake had expected, the questions were starting to bubble out from Alice.

"So why aren't I frozen as well? How come I'm still moving?"

"It's because you were touching me at the instant I stopped time. When Fergus jumped off the ledge, you grabbed my arm just as I clicked my fingers. If I'm touching anyone when I stop time, then they're immune too. It was just pure coincidence that you grabbed me at that moment, and I couldn't do anything about it."

"So when did you become a Timekeeper – and how?" she asked.

"Only a few months ago. Mr Walker passed his powers on to me before he died."

"Mr Walker? So he really was a Timekeeper like Fergus said?"

"Yes."

"That explains the house, then."

This conversation could take hours, he thought. Despite being frozen in time, he needed to concentrate on the current situation. Alice's presence was a complication that had to be taken into account, but he couldn't allow it to become a distraction.

"Look, Alice, it's a long story. It's also really important that it remains a secret. Nobody is meant to know about the Timekeepers but, since you've found out, I'll tell you about it later. Right now we've got to figure out what to do about Fergus."

Alice looked over the wall again. "Yeah, you're right," she said. "Can you save him?"

"Oh, saving him is the easy part," he said. "The difficult part comes later on if he decides to publish a story about all this."

"So what are you going to do?"

Jake thought about it. "I need some help from a colleague."

"You mean there are other Timekeepers too?"

It was understandable, but everything he said prompted another question from Alice.

"Yes. Look, just give me a minute to think about it," he said. She remained silent, and looked down at the High Street again.

Jake was in turmoil. It was one thing Alice finding out about his secret – and, if pressed, he would probably confess to being pleased about that – but what about the Traveller? He'd be very unimpressed, wouldn't he? And the Master would probably be angry too. It might not have been his fault, but Jake had still let them down, and the secret had been revealed to a family member. What was he going to do?

He could start and stop time quickly. That would freeze Alice, and he could then call for help from the Traveller. But, in the split second that it would take to start and stop time again, Fergus would drop another couple of feet and he'd be out of their reach. That would make it more difficult to address the situation. No, he'd have to call the Traveller, and face up to the fact that Alice knew the secret. It would be better to be honest about it. Besides, it had hardly been deliberate. And if the Traveller thought that Alice was a risk, he could get Retro to take them back to the time just before Fergus jumped. The secret would be intact, and Alice would never know. But he hoped that the Traveller wouldn't do that.

He sighed. Only one way to find out, he thought.

He pulled out the pocket watch.

"What are you doing?" asked Alice.

"I'm calling my colleague – he's called the Traveller," Jake explained.

"You're calling him? Shouldn't you use your phone?"

"No, we use pocket watches like this one. You remember when Mr Walker gave this to me? He gave you that crystal clock."

"Oh yes, I remember. So you use the pocket watch to contact a *traveller*?"

"That's his title – the Traveller."

"Title?" said Alice. "Have you got a title too?"

"Yes," said Jake. "I'm called the Freezer."

Alice laughed. "The Freezer? What sort of name is that?"

Jake smiled. It did sound slightly ridiculous, unless you were a Timekeeper. "It's simple, I can freeze time, so I'm called the Freezer. Now, please, let me call the Traveller."

He pushed down on the crown with his thumb and turned half of the minute hand to the number two. He let go, and the Traveller appeared

143

in an instant. Alice jumped in alarm, and the Traveller stepped back with a look of surprise on his face. Both of them looked at Jake.

"Erm – Traveller, this is my sister Alice," said Jake weakly.

The Traveller composed himself surprisingly quickly. "A pleasure to meet you, Alice," he said with a warm smile that put Alice at ease instantly.

"Yeah, you too," said Alice.

There was a pause.

"Um – excuse me, Alice. I need a word with Jake." Without waiting for her response, he put an arm around Jake's shoulders, turned him around and steered him away from Alice so that she couldn't hear.

"There's an explanation for this, I trust?" He spoke quietly, but didn't seem as angry as Jake had expected him to be. Perhaps he was waiting to hear what Jake had to say before he made up his mind.

"She grabbed my arm at precisely the moment I stopped time," said Jake. "By the time I realised what had happened, it was too late."

"Too late?" He looked around the empty car park. "We seem to be standing on the roof of a multi storey car park, and there's nobody else up here, so what gave you away? Even I can't tell the difference at the moment."

"No, but then you haven't looked over the wall yet," said Jake.

"And what's over there?"

"Fergus – about two feet down, suspended in mid air after he jumped."

"Ah." He walked over to the wall and looked over, then turned back to Jake. "Yes, I see what you mean. God, is that man ever going to leave us alone?"

"If I start time again, he certainly will," said Jake.

The Traveller laughed. "Yes, but I don't think that's really an option, is it?"

"No, not really," said Jake.

"So what's Fergus doing there? Why did he jump?"

Jake told him about Fergus' plan, and what he had said before he jumped. The Traveller was amazed.

"You mean, he jumped off here just to prove – by you saving him – that the Timekeepers actually exist? He must be mad."

"But he's not, is he?" said Jake. "He knows it, and we know it. He knows enough about the Timekeepers to know that we wouldn't let him die, especially if I was standing here when he jumped. It's a pretty radical way of testing us, though."

"It certainly is. He must have either been very confident or very stupid." The Traveller looked back down at Fergus. "Thing is, what do we do about it? We've got to save him, but what will he do next?"

"Excuse me," said Alice. They had forgotten about her, standing there in silence whilst they had been discussing the situation. They both turned to her.

"I was thinking," she continued. "If Fergus wanted to prove that the Timekeepers exist, wouldn't he do something like set up a video of all this so he has evidence on film?"

The Traveller looked at Jake. "Smart sister you've got there, Jake. Yes, I think he would have done something like that. Alice, why don't you go and have a look around to see if you can find any cameras? If you find one, though, please don't touch it. Just let us know."

"Sure." Pleased that she was no longer just a silent spectator, Alice set off.

The Traveller turned back to Jake.

"You'd better tell me how much she knows," he said. "Otherwise it'll be difficult for us to discuss anything in front of her. She might have found out by accident, but that doesn't mean that she should know any more than she really needs to."

Jake nodded. "Of course," he said. "She really doesn't know much. I had to tell her that I was a Timekeeper, and that I'd inherited my powers from Mr Walker. And I had to tell her about you of course, but I haven't mentioned any of the others. But she's bound to have loads of questions later, though. What should I do?"

"Let's wait until this is over first, then we can discuss it properly. I'll need to think about it for a while. So, what shall we do about dear old Fergus?"

Jake walked over and looked down.

"I think we're lucky so far. Fergus didn't make a sound when he jumped, and it doesn't look as though anybody is looking up this way. It's unlikely that he'd be seen to disappear if we moved him, which is a relief."

"Okay, but then what?"

Jake thought about it. Whatever they did, Fergus would know about it. After all, he had planned it like that. They couldn't put anything underneath Fergus to break his fall: it would look odd if a pile of boxes or other things suddenly appeared at the bottom of the car park, and there was no guarantee that they would work effectively anyway.

Jake's thoughts were interrupted by Alice running over.

"There's a video camera on a small tripod over in the far corner. It's been surrounded by some boxes and rags to make it look like rubbish, but there's a video camera inside, pointing in this direction."

"Well done, Alice," said the Traveller. "That makes our job much easier. I'll go and have a look at it once we've decided what we're going to do. Just have one more scout around to see if there are any others, will you?"

"Okay." Alice went off again at a trot. Jake thought it was quite clever how the Traveller had managed to get Alice out of earshot again by making her feel so useful.

The Traveller turned back to Jake. "So, any ideas?"

"Only one," said Jake. "Let's just bring him back up here, so he falls on the floor. That will obviously give him the confirmation he's looking for that we exist, but that might not be such a bad thing."

"Eh? How do you figure that?"

"Well, he'll know that I've really got the powers that he thinks I have. I can use that to scare him." Jake was thinking about it as he talked. He wasn't sure if it would work, but the options were limited. "Perhaps I can tell him that yes, he's right about the Timekeepers. I'll say that there are three of us — he said he heard two or three voices in the park toilets. But I can tell him that we'll only save him if he promises never to print another word about us."

"You reckon that would work?"

"It's worth a try," said Jake. "Besides, we haven't got any other options really, have we? And we've have the video tape anyway, so he couldn't use that."

Alice came back to them. "I've searched everywhere. I couldn't see any other cameras."

"Good," said the Traveller. "He went to so much trouble to hide the first video camera, I didn't think there'd be another. Show us where the camera is, and we'll get the tape out."

Alice took them over to the hidden tripod, and the Traveller inspected the camera. It was focussed on the spot where Fergus had jumped, and it was switched to record. Presumably Fergus didn't need to record himself actually falling: it would be enough to show that he had jumped off the building. Retrieving the tape and showing that he was still very much alive would be evidence enough to prove that something had happened, even if the video didn't show exactly what the Timekeepers were doing.

The Traveller opened the camera and removed the tape. He passed it to Jake.

"Here," he said, "you'll need this for when you speak to Fergus."

They started walking back to where Fergus was hanging.

"So have you decided what to do?" asked Alice, still slightly out of breath from running all over the car park.

"I think so," said the Traveller. "Jake, do it your way. Let me know if you need any help, otherwise I'll wait to hear from you later. Alice, please do exactly as Jake says. Don't speak to Fergus or interfere in any way, whatever happens. That's really important, okay?" Alice nodded. "Also, I hope I don't need to remind you that you never mention a word about any of this to anyone. The secret of the Timekeepers is paramount – you just need to look at Fergus to see the trouble it causes when somebody tries to expose us. So please, not a word to anyone, ever. Can I trust you to respect that wish?"

Alice looked serious, as if she had only just realised just how important all this was. She looked at Jake, and then back to the Traveller.

"Yes, I promise," she said.

"Good girl," said the Traveller. "Now, Jake, let's get Fergus back up here and I'll let you get on with it."

The two of them reached over the wall and each grabbed a part of Fergus' clothes. Jake had the trouser belt, and the Traveller had the collar. Between them, they pulled him up and over the wall, and left him hanging only a foot or so above the ground. That might even be enough to shock him into silence anyway, thought Jake. He tried to imagine what it would be like for Fergus to be facing such a huge drop and, in a split second, be only a foot above the ground.

Jake brushed himself down and took out the pocket watch. He pushed down the crown and reunited the two halves of the minute hand. He nodded at the Traveller, who nodded back, and he released the crown. The Traveller disappeared instantly.

Alice was stunned, and looked all around her. "Spooky," she said. "Does that happen often?"

"Only when it's necessary for us to meet," said Jake as he put the pocket watch away. "Right, let's get on with it. Remember, let me do all the talking, okay?"

"Okay," she agreed.

"Just so you know," he said, "I'm going to click my fingers again and time will restart. In that instant, Fergus will hit the floor here. He won't hurt himself, although he's likely to be very surprised."

"He'll also be very wet, since you've put him over a puddle," Alice pointed out.

Jake grinned. "I hadn't noticed that, but it's a nice touch. Better than being splattered all over the pavement down there anyway."

"Yurgh – I don't even want to think about that," said Alice.

"Anyway, I'm not quite sure what'll happen after that. It depends on how Fergus reacts. But don't get involved, okay?"

She nodded.

"Right, let's do it."

Click!

CHAPTER TWENTY ONE

Fergus squealed as he hit the ground with a splash. His arms and legs flailed around as he realised he was still alive, but he looked like a fish out of water. The shock on his face was evident. It was almost comical to watch.

He spluttered and shook his face. After a few moments, he regained his composure and looked up to see Jake standing next to him. He got up on to his knees and then stood, a bit shakily, brushing water and dirt from his front.

"Ah, Jake," he said. He tried a smile, but Jake's face was rigid, and the smile faded. He looked over the wall. "My goodness, that was a close one. Still, I have to say that I'm most relieved to have been proved right."

"That was such a stupid thing to do," said Jake sternly.

"Possibly, yes," said Fergus, "but that was precisely the point. I had to find out whether my confidence in you was well-placed. Fortunately, it was. I knew you'd save me, you didn't have a choice."

"Oh, but I did," replied Jake. "In fact, I thought about it long and hard."

To Jake's satisfaction, Fergus actually looked shocked. "What? You'd have let me fall to my death?" He obviously hadn't considered that possibility beforehand.

"Think about it," he said. "If I'd let you die, you'd no longer have been a threat to me. I could have been miles away by the time you'd hit the ground, and there's no way the police could have connected me to the scene. Look at you – you're a failure, nobody believes your stuff about the Timekeepers, you've lost all credibility as a journalist, you're a loner. They're classic circumstances for committing suicide, and that would have suited me just fine. I'd never have to worry about whether you'd print another article, and I could get on with my life. Besides, you hounded Mr Walker about being a Timekeeper, and that stress might have contributed to his death. I hate you for that, if nothing else. No, in some ways I would have been happy to let you fall."

The truth must have hurt. Fergus looked down at the ground and, just for an instant, he looked thoroughly ashamed of himself. He muttered something to himself and looked back at Jake defiantly.

"But I'm right," he said. "I'm right. You wouldn't admit it, so I had to get confirmation of it some other way. If only you had admitted it earlier – or Mr Walker, for that matter – it wouldn't have come to this." His tone became less defensive. "And don't flatter yourself, Jake. If I had died, the police could easily have placed you at the scene. I made sure of that, just as a precaution."

Jake produced the video tape from his jacket and held it up.

"What, with this?" he said. "Did you think I wouldn't find it?"

"Give that back," snapped Fergus viciously. He stepped forward and reached out for the tape.

Click!

Fergus froze in mid stride.

Jake put the tape on the ground, just in front of Fergus' raised foot, and stamped on it hard. The case splintered, and he ground the tape into the water and grime, ensuring that it was beyond repair. Then he returned to his original position.

Click!

Fergus' hand snatched through thin air as his foot crunched the ruined tape in the puddle under his foot. He looked at Jake's empty hand, and then down at the ground. Amazement turned to anger.

"Why, you – " He raised his fist and aimed it at Jake's face. Alice screamed.

Click!

Jake walked past Fergus and stood a few feet behind him, with his back to the wall.

Click!

Fergus stumbled forward and fell to his knees. He spun around and stood up, facing Jake with a look of fury on his face. Again, he lunged forward.

Click!

Again, Jake went and stood several feet behind Fergus, beyond his reach. He checked on Alice, but she seemed to look less scared now. She could see that Jake had the upper hand.

Click!

Fergus stopped and spun round again. He was breathing heavily, a look of hatred in his eyes. He stood still for a moment.

"You see?" said Jake calmly. "You can't touch me now. I can do things in front of you that I couldn't do before, and there's nothing you can do about it."

"I'll still get you for this," spat Fergus. "I'm not finished, not yet."

"Yes, you are," said Jake. "This ends here, and now. I want your word that you'll leave me alone, and that you'll never print another article about the Timekeepers."

Fergus laughed.

"You're kidding, right?"

Jake felt brazen. "Do I look like I'm kidding?"

"You've just given me more material than I ever thought possible, and you expect me just to give it up now?"

"That's right."

"And if I don't?" Fergus was still defiant, and Jake was ready for him to attempt another assault.

"If you don't," he said, "I'll take you back in time to the moment when you're suspended in mid air on the other side of that wall. Then I start time again. Easy."

"You wouldn't allow me to die," he scoffed.

"I hope that won't be necessary," said Jake. "But I've got to protect the secret, and I'll do whatever that takes."

"Including murder?" said Fergus.

"Oh no, not murder, but it would be suicide anyway. You jumped, remember? Nobody pushed you, or even touched you. It's just that, next time, I wouldn't be here to stop you."

"And what if I agree not to publish any more articles?"

"Then you'll never hear from me again. But you have to promise, and I'll know if you're not telling the truth."

Fergus looked confused. "How's that?"

"You already know I've got a couple of – let's say colleagues," said Jake. "If you were to promise now that you would never print another word about us, I could have that checked within five minutes. One of my colleagues is very clever: they can see what happens in the future."

"They can?" Fergus was almost dribbling at the thought of what it would do for him as a journalist if he exposed and proved that.

"Yes, so that means we can easily check to see whether you're telling the truth or not, and if you're not..." He left the sentence unfinished for Fergus to draw his own conclusions.

"Yes," said Fergus slowly. "I do believe you can." Jake could see the realisation dawn on Fergus' face that he had nowhere else to go. His shoulders dropped, and he slumped to the ground, sitting against the wall. Jake let him wallow in self pity for a few moments, but then he felt a stab of guilt.

"Look," he said, "you've achieved what you set out to achieve. You've proved beyond all doubt that Timekeepers exist. You should be proud of that. The amount of time and effort you've put into proving it – well, it hasn't all been wasted, has it?"

Fergus looked up at him. He was sad, deflated, beaten.

"No, I suppose not," he said quietly.

"The only problem is that you can't write about it. You can't use the story. That doesn't make you a bad journalist, does it? At least you've proved that you can get to the bottom of a story without giving up."

"For all the good *that's* done me," muttered Fergus bitterly.

"Couldn't you help each other?" asked Alice. She hadn't uttered a word since Fergus had been saved, and Jake had forgotten she was there. He looked at her sharply.

"What?"

"I don't know," said Alice. "But look, I've only just discovered that you're a Timekeeper, Jake. Fergus is a journalist, and he knows about you too now. He's not allowed to write any articles about it, and that's fine – as you said, the secret must be protected. But couldn't you two try to work together?"

"What – you mean work with Fergus?" asked Jake, surprised at the suggestion.

Fergus was quicker on the uptake. He stood up and looked at Alice.

"Do you know, young lady, I think you might be on to something there."

"Now hold on a second – " said Jake.

"No, Jake, just listen to me for a minute," said Alice crossly. "I've stood here quietly like you told me, and I've watched you two squabbling and Fergus trying to hit you. Wouldn't it be easier to work together instead of arguing all the time? You can stop time, and Fergus is a journalist. You could give him some great stories, couldn't you? After all, he's spent years chasing the Timekeepers, and what's he got to show for it after all that time? Nothing. He's a wreck, but it's not his fault, is it? The least you could do is help get his career back. And in return, it's more likely that Fergus will keep his promise not to write any more articles on the Timekeepers."

Fergus looked from Jake to Alice, and back again.

"You know," he said, "that's an extraordinarily sensible idea coming from one so young as you. What do you think, Jake?"

Jake was torn. Actually, the idea made perfect sense to him – he wished he'd thought of it himself. But what would the others say? It was true that Fergus would be more likely to keep his word and, after all, he had been right about the Timekeepers all along. Yes, it broke the code of silence surrounding the secret, but what else could be done? Both Alice and Fergus now knew about the Timekeepers, even if they only knew a little bit. Of course that would increase the risk of others finding out, but what was the alternative? Alice and Fergus would both have to be taken back in time, but then Fergus would still be on their case all the time. A pact between them must be sensible.

"I don't have that sort of authority," he said. "I'd have to consult the – my colleagues."

"Of course you should," said Fergus. "Um, and how do you do that?"

Jake smiled at him. "Always the journalist, Fergus!"

Fergus grinned sheepishly. "Well, of course, I'd be fascinated to know," he said.

"Let's get one thing straight," said Jake. "Whatever happens, I'm not going to reveal any more to you than the bare minimum. The more you know, the less safe the secret is. That stands to reason, doesn't it?"

Fergus conceded. "I suppose so, but you can't blame me for trying."

"Well, I'd stop trying if I were you. We're not working together yet, and the others might not agree anyway. So I'll see what they say. Just give me a minute."

Click!

Jake pulled the pocket watch out and turned half of the minute hand to the number two. The Traveller appeared instantly.

"We meet again so soon, Jake," he said. "That bad, eh?"

"Not too bad, actually. But I need to call a meeting of the Timekeepers."

"When, now?"

"Is that possible?"

"Possible yes, but a little unusual. If it's that urgent, shouldn't you call everybody here instead?"

"I thought of that," said Jake, "but I need the Master's opinion too. I think it would be better if we had a formal meeting."

"Alright," said the Traveller. "I'll contact the others. You go to the meeting room and we'll join you there shortly. You'll need to reunite the minute hand first before setting it on the number six."

"Yes, of course. Thanks."

Jake reunited the minute hand, and the Traveller vanished.

Click!

He started time again, since the Traveller would need to talk to all of the Timekeepers in turn to prepare the meeting. Neither Fergus nor Alice had noticed anything unusual.

"I've called a meeting with the others," he said.

"When did you do that?" asked Fergus.

"Just now."

"But you didn't do anything. You didn't move."

"No, Fergus, you didn't *see* me move. There's a difference."

Fergus was amazed. "What, in that split second, you called a meeting? How?"

"No more questions, please," said Jake. "As I said, there's a lot you don't know, and it will probably stay that way, whatever the other say. I'm going to the meeting now, but you won't notice that either." Confusion played over their faces, but Jake liked that. It keeps them on their toes, he thought.

He looked at his watch. That should be enough time, he thought.

Click!

He pulled out the pocket watch again, and carefully turned half of the minute hand round to the number six. When he released the crown, he vanished.

CHAPTER TWENTY TWO

Once again, Jake found himself standing in that familiar white, windowless room with strange lighting. He was first to arrive, but the others followed almost at once. Most of them looked a little dishevelled, and had clearly not been ready for a meeting at such short notice. When his five colleagues were assembled, the Master appeared. Unlike the others, he always looked fresh and prepared.

"So, Freezer," he said in his calm deep voice, "you have gathered us together to discuss a matter of deep importance, I understand."

"Yes, Master," said Jake. "And I must first of all apologise to you, and to my colleagues, for asking the Traveller to convene us so quickly. I hope the urgency will become clear to everybody after you have heard what I have to say."

"If I was mortal, I would be intrigued," said the Master with a wry smile. "Please go on."

Jake took a deep breath to compose himself.

"Thank you, Master," he said. "You will know that we have an ongoing – er – situation with Fergus Dingley. This afternoon, he tried to commit suicide in front of me – " There was a collective gasp from Retro, Seeker and Splitter. " – in the knowledge that I would save him. He wanted to prove that I was a Timekeeper, and he was convinced that I couldn't let him die. The Traveller and I saved him but, in doing that, we acknowledged that Fergus was right. He had tried to record the incident on video, but I destroyed the tape. He got very aggressive, and I told him that we could not allow him to print any further articles about the Timekeepers. He has seen the powers that I have, but he still doesn't know much else about the Timekeepers. I told him that we would allow him to live only if he promised never to write another article about us, and said that we could easily check the future to know if his promise remained intact."

"That seems an eminently sensible suggestion," interrupted the Master. "And how did he respond?"

"Well, Master, he didn't respond immediately. I think he was trying to figure out if there was any way in which he could profit from his new knowledge about my powers, especially now that he had seen it with his own eyes. But my sister – "

"Your sister, Freezer?" said the Master.

"Yes, Master. My sister Alice grabbed my arm at the same time I clicked my fingers after Fergus jumped. She knows too, I'm afraid. There was really nothing I could do about it until it was too late."

"That seems a bit careless, Jake," said the Master. "Two mortals discovering your powers in the course of one afternoon." It was only a mild rebuke, but to Jake it felt like a javelin through the heart.

"If I may speak, Master?" said the Traveller. The Master nodded. "I am satisfied that it was purely coincidental that Alice grabbed Jake's arm at such an unfortunate moment. Such an action was understandable, in the circumstances. As for Fergus – well, I believe we must all share the blame for that. We did not check thoroughly enough before stripping him of his powers, and it has been a risk that Freezer and his predecessor had to manage to the best of their abilities. It was inevitable, I think, that Fergus would someday learn more about the truth. It has been something of a lifelong quest for him."

"Indeed, you are right, Traveller," said the Master. He turned back to Jake. "Freezer, it is a fact that your powers are always going to be more prone to discovery than those of your other colleagues here. There is a constant risk that someone will notice even the slightest of movements. It is not the same for those who can travel forwards or backwards in time, or be in two places at once. They can usually choose to do that when the risk of discovery is minimal, or when you have already frozen time. You have done well to protect the secret so far, and you deserve no criticism. I do not blame you for it. Nonetheless, I lament the fact that some aspects of the secret are now known to others – which of course increases the risk to all of us."

Jake inwardly heaved a sigh of relief, although he didn't feel as though he was out of the woods yet. He still had to come to the point of the meeting. His heart was pounding as he continued.

"Thank you, Master," he said. "Since assuming my role as Freezer, I have always been aware that protection of the secret is paramount. Since being stripped of his powers, Fergus has always been the biggest risk to our security. He has been determined to expose us, and now he knows beyond all doubt that I am a Timekeeper." He paused briefly to take a deep breath, and he looked around the circle at his colleagues. "I think we could make a deal with him."

There was a moment of silence.

"A deal?" said the Master.

Jake knew that he had to tread carefully.

"He might promise not to write any more articles about us. I told him that, if he did, I could take him back in time to the point when he had just jumped of the top of the car park, but I don't think he took me seriously. He knew that I couldn't be responsible for his death: as a Timekeeper, we're meant to save lives, rather than destroy them. But, in a way, we have already destroyed Fergus' life, haven't we? It might have been alright if he hadn't left himself that note before being stripped of his powers, but that's when his life started going wrong. Nobody believed him, but he had to know the truth. And in doing that, he ruined himself. So I thought, why can't we help him, instead of destroy him? None of this is really his fault, is it? And, if we help him, it's far more likely that he would keep his promise never to print another article about the Timekeepers."

Jake paused, and looked around the room for a reaction. He knew that none of them had any reason to trust Fergus. He didn't have any real reason himself, but his instinct told him that Alice was right. It would be better to work with Fergus than fight him.

The Master inclined his head to one side and looked enquiringly at Jake from beneath the hood.

"What type of help did you have in mind, Freezer?"

At least he didn't reject the idea immediately, Jake thought. The others waited for Jake to respond.

"He's a journalist, and we are Timekeepers. We could feed him some great stories, and I suppose he could let us know if there's something we could help with too. It might just give him a chance to get back on his feet again. Don't we owe him that?"

There was silence.

Jake was disappointed. Maybe it was a stupid idea after all, he thought. Maybe he hadn't thought it through properly.

The silence was broken by Splitter. "I agree," he said.

Jake felt a glimmer of hope.

"Me too," said Seeker. "Sometimes I just don't have time to keep an eye on what's going on. I think it could work well."

The Master looked at both of them, and then back to Jake, who was holding his breath so tightly that he thought his lungs might burst. The Master held up his hand, indicating that no further comment was required from the others.

"It is a sensible suggestion, Freezer."

Jake let the air escape from his chest as quietly as he could, but the enormous relief on his face was hard to miss.

"However – "

Jake drew another sharp breath in, and bit his lower lip as he waited for the Master to go on.

"However, I think it would be prudent, this time, to make quite sure that Fergus keeps to his word. Seeker, Traveller, I want both of you to search well. If you find even the slightest indication that any further articles are written, then I cannot agree. We will wait for you."

The Traveller nodded, and walked across the circle to the Seeker. They linked arms, and vanished.

The Master looked at Jake.

"Fergus has caused us much anxiety over the years," he said, "and we cannot afford to let that continue. The Traveller was right when he said that we must accept some of the blame for Fergus' actions. Your proposal is a bold one, but I agree that cooperation is better than strife. For that reason, I hope this search reveals nothing that might cause me concern."

Jake nodded, but remained quiet. There was nothing he could say until the Traveller and the Seeker returned.

Fortunately, he didn't have to wait long. Having reappeared, they separated and returned to their original places in the circle.

"Master," said the Traveller. "We have looked at every possible angle, but found nothing to suggest that Fergus breaks his promise. I am confident that he will keep his word."

Jake felt a great weight lift from his shoulders. He looked at the Master, who smiled.

"Freezer, once again you have impressed me with your maturity. I am content for you to proceed as you suggest. I take it that other colleagues have no objection to that?"

There was silence around the circle.

"But be careful, Freezer. Your grip on Fergus must always be tight. We cannot afford to let the secret become known to others. As for Alice..." He paused, and Jake's heart missed a beat. "...I see no reason to take her back in time. But again, you must impress upon her the weight of the responsibility she now bears."

"Thank you, Master," said Jake. "I will do my best."

"Of that, I have no doubt. Traveller – I trust that you will maintain a close interest in this issue?" The Traveller bowed his head in agreement.

"Retro, Seeker, Splitter. It is in all our interests to ensure that, from this time on, Fergus remains a friend rather than a foe. But he should not be informed of your existence, and your assistance should be channelled through Freezer. We do indeed owe him a life, but he must help himself too. It will be up to Freezer to make that clear to him." He looked around the circle to check that his instructions were clear. Each Timekeeper in turn met his eyes and nodded. "And so, until our next meeting, I bid you farewell, my friends." He bowed his head and vanished.

The remainder of the circle disintegrated as they mingled.

"Good idea, Jake," said the Seeker. "I reckon I can keep Fergus busy for a long time, if he's keen."

"Thanks, Annie," said Jake. "I'm sure he'll be grateful."

"In fact," she said, "I was cruising around just before we came here. There's going to be a train crash in a couple of days. We can make sure nobody gets hurt, but it'll be a good one for Fergus to cover."

The Seeker gave him the details.

"I reckon Jake's had enough for one day," said the Traveller. "Let's get together and sort out the train crash tomorrow, okay?" Everyone agreed. "I'll call you."

Jake shook hands with Splitter and the Traveller, and hugged Retro and Seeker. They all took out their pocket watches and reunited the minute hand. One by one, they disappeared. Jake found himself once again on the roof of the multi storey car park. He had to think hard about the position in which he had been standing before he had stopped time.

Click!

"How long will it take?" asked Fergus.

"How long will what take?" said Jake.

"The meeting. I'm getting cold up here."

"Oh, I've just been."

"You what? When?"

"Just now. I told you, you wouldn't notice."

Fergus and Alice exchanged glances.

"Yeah, right," said Alice sarcastically, "like you've been anywhere!"

Jake sighed. "Well, you two are going to have to get used to that."

"What – you mean...?" said Fergus.

"Yes," said Jake with a broad grin. "The Ma – er – my colleagues have agreed that we can work together."

"Excellent," said Fergus. "But what does that mean in practice?"

"It means that, from time to time, I will be able to let you know about any breaking news stories. As a journalist, it's up to you to turn that into front page exclusives."

Fergus' jaw dropped open. "Front page exclusives? You mean, national paper stuff?"

"That's right," said Jake, reeling him in. A dreamy look came over Fergus' face. "And in return, you can let me know if there's anything with which the Timekeepers might be able to help."

"How do you mean?"

"It's what we do — saving lives, protecting the innocent. Once you've got a decent job, you'll be able to keep an eye on what's going on, and you can call me if you think I'd be able to help. But there's one condition, of course."

"Name it."

"You are never — and I mean never — to print any further articles about the Timekeepers, or our activities. You must never even mention what you know to another living soul."

Fergus thought about it for a minute, then shrugged his shoulders. "You know, exposing the Timekeepers was the only front page exclusive I've ever really chased. But, hey, if you can offer me other top stories on a plate, who am I to refuse?"

"I'm really serious about this, Fergus. I need to know that you'll keep your word."

Fergus looked him in the eye. "Alright," he said. "You have my word. I promise." He held out his hand, and Jake took it.

"Friends?" said Fergus as they shook hands.

"You know what?" said Jake, smiling. "I think we will be."

"Well, it's about time," said Alice.

They both looked at her. "Pardon?" said Jake.

"It's about time you two became friends. Fergus doesn't have to jump off buildings any more, and Jake can stop worrying about any articles about the Timekeepers. Simple, really, wasn't it? So can we go home now, please? It's freezing up here."

Jake and Fergus looked at each other and smiled.

"Yeah, alright," said Jake. He started walking off, and then remembered and turned back. "Oh, Fergus, I almost forgot. Get down to London and buy yourself a ticket for the 1035 express train to Glasgow on Thursday. Sit in the front carriage."

Fergus frowned. "Why?"

"It's going to crash," said Jake.

"What?" he spluttered. "And you want me on it?"

Jake rolled his eyes. "It's okay, nobody gets hurt. We'll make sure of that. But if you're in the front carriage when it crashes, you've got your first front page exclusive, haven't you?"

Slowly, Fergus smiled. "Oh, yes," he said. "Yes, yes, yes!"

Jake held up his hand to calm him down. "But not a word to anybody else, right?"

"You got it," said Fergus. He danced around, punching the air in triumph. "My first exclusive – yes!"

Jake turned back to Alice, shaking his head.

"Where did we leave our bags?"

"Over at the top of the stairs."

"Come on then, let's go home. We've got a lot to talk about. On the way, I'll tell you about Mr Walker."

THE END

Printed in the United Kingdom
by Lightning Source UK Ltd.
108526UKS00001B/190-204